I0450955

HENRY AND ANNE

BARB JONES

This is a work of fiction. Names, characters, places, and incidents are products of the author's imagination or are used fictitiously and are not to be construed as real. Any resemblance to actual events, locations, organizations, or persons, living or dead, is entirely coincidental.

World Castle Publishing, LLC
Pensacola, Florida
Copyright © Barb Jones 2022
Hardback ISBN: 9798832242828
Paperback ISBN: 9781958336151
eBook ISBN: 9781958336168
First Edition World Castle Publishing, LLC, June 20, 2022.
http://www.worldcastlepublishing.com

Licensing Notes

All rights reserved. No part of this book may be used or reproduced in any manner whatsoever without written permission, except in the case of brief quotations embodied in articles and reviews.

Cover: Karen Fuller
Editor: Maxine Bringenberg

Acknowledgment

I have always loved the Tudor legacy, and Anne of Cleves is my favorite of his six wives. I wrote this novel to give Anne something she missed by only being married to Henry for six months—love and independence. Something different for that time period. Anne never married again, remained in England, and was loved by her household, among many others. It is said she was always kind but often lonely as well. She survived a marriage to Henry while other queens did not. Henry VIII is known for his six wives, and two of them were beheaded. It has been a topic of many scholars that she was one of his more successful wives, allowed to live out her life maintaining the king's friendship and love. Anne was the most admired and successful wife. She needed to win Henry over to stay in England. When Henry remarried, she remained in his good graces and was always welcomed at court.

This is fictional except for the pieces of history regarding the lives of Henry VIII and Anne of Cleves. Her life is not well-documented after the annulment. But her newfound status quo as the King's Beloved Sister and the favor he gave her once she agreed were impeccable. She would be afforded the same respect given to the queen of England and his daughters, Princess Mary and Princess Elizabeth.

I hope you enjoy reading this as much as I have enjoyed writing it and creating the life for Anne of Cleves that I wish she could have had.

Prologue

Richmond, July 1, 1540

My lady-in-waiting, Mary Arundell, was in the middle of making her play in chess when the door to the queen's rooms opened. Henry walked in and said in a commanding voice, "Leave, all of you, save the queen and her great Lady Mary, Countess of Sussex." Turning to a servant, he said, "Bring us wine and cheese."

As I saw my rooms empty of all persons but the king, my lady, and me, I couldn't help but admire Henry's strength in his rule. I'd lived in England around seven months, married to this pompous man, but in that time, I learned not only my place as his queen but what he desired. Hastily I prepared a place for Henry to sit. Giving him a place of honor and strength allowed him to open up to me. I proved my worth by always listening and offering my consolation or advice only when he asked for it. Although I knew I was not pleasing to

His Majesty, I was still his queen consort, if in name only. In fact, I knew the real reason I was sent from court to Richmond regarding the king's eye, but I still maintained my dignity and obeyed his wishes. At least he came to visit in secret. I fluffed one of the feathered pillows and placed it on a footstool, allowing His Majesty to lift his feet. I asked my lady to fetch a blanket from the inner rooms and set it aside in case there was a draft.

"Your Majesty, I am pleased to have you visit me this evening. But, by your command, I sense there is something you wish to speak of…in private?"

"Yes, Anne. When Lady Mary returns, we will begin a most helpful discussion. I think you will learn to see things my way."

Henry sat in the chair I'd made comfortable for him and waited for the servant to return with the wine and cheese. The servant entered and set up the serving tray for all in attendance. There were three gold goblets and three plates with cheese, breads, and grapes. This would be a long discussion. Henry, in his forty-eighth year, was a man that showed no signs of slowing down, but his weight was on the increase, and he experienced problems with his feet periodically. Though he showed no signs of outward pain, he was a man that kept his thoughts private. Since coming to England earlier that year, I had made significant strides in getting Henry to open his thoughts to me, even if just a little.

I sat in the chair to his right and kept my hands busy with needlepoint until he was ready. Occasionally I would glance up and notice either him taking a sip of wine, eating a piece of cheese, or even sneaking a glance my way. Lady

Mary sat to the other side of me, but behind me, given her place in my court. Considering I'd lost most of my ladies once I arrived in King Henry's court, I was thankful for Lady Mary's tutelage and friendship.

Henry was growing restless with the quiet. I knew not to anger him in this mood. I knew from my brother, Duke Wilhelm Cleves, that Henry was the most athletic man, tall and broad shouldered in his younger years, but several years ago, he'd suffered an injury that transformed this once beautiful man into a man that my ladies called "a fat smelly king" when no one was around listening to them speak. But whenever I looked into his eyes, I could see that same young man that was known for his looks, physique, and insatiable appetite for food, wine, and women. He was still young at heart. His red hair still had a shimmer of gold in it, his smile could light up a room, and his voice could bend anyone to his will despite his temper and mood. Henry was still the same Henry despite his ulcers, obesity, and his infamous nature for his many wives. I was, as the cooks in the kitchens would joke, the fourth wife, and bets were placed on how long I could keep my head attached to my body.

"Lady Mary, can you scribe, or shall we fetch another?" asked the king.

"Aye, Your Majesty. I can scribe. May I get what I need for your request?"

Henry nodded, and as my lady rose from her sewing, he lingered a glance on her form as she went to the desk and retrieved what was needed. A smile rose from his lips, and he muttered, "Damn, the count is one lucky man to ride that mare." I knew of Henry's commentary on the ladies in the court and paid it no mind, as I wished to keep my head intact.

"Anne, have some wine. This will open the discussion."

"Yes, my lord. I noticed there were three goblets. Are we waiting for someone else?"

"No, the third is for your great Lady Mary. This is a serious discussion that must remain between us, and I need a witness. Do you understand, Anne?"

I nodded in obedience and attended to the king's wishes. Lady Mary and I were waiting in silence for the king to be at ease. Yet the silence remained. I reflected on not only being in court but on my education of the English court under his rule prior to the marriage. A small smile escaped from my lips, though I remained in silence.

I knew my place was to marry the king of England, despite the stories of him being much older, obese, and a hard-drinking man who was well known for divorcing or beheading his wives when they displeased him. I learned obedience from my father and mother but longed to escape the reality that my brother kept me prisoner in. So I agreed to marry this so-called fat king. When I had met him in private in Rochester, I knew this marriage would not last long, but I still honored the alliance that was made in exchange for my body. Even though I pleaded with my brother that I was not educated in music, reading, or the arts to keep a husband's attention, I was educated in the affairs of politics itself. My brother, as cold as he could always be, reminded me that my purpose in a marriage was for the political alliances it would bring to the Cleves.

King Henry, from the moment we first met, made me aware that I did not please him with my body, but I took from that my opportunity to make him content with my mind and soul. I listened when he needed an ear. I played games with him to keep his mind off the pain and allowed him the fancy to take pleasures elsewhere while not going against him. Both Henry and I knew our marriage wasn't consummated, but that was never public knowledge. It is not a woman's place to test her husband's virility or share secrets of the bedchamber with others outside the marriage. We never discussed his moments of impotence when he tried to get me with an heir to protect the royal line. Instead, I endured the court gossip of my ugly looks preventing me from conceiving, and on nights he could perform, he took pleasures from one lady in the court with my secret consent. In return, when Henry would visit my chambers, only my great Lady Mary stayed in presence while we either played a game of chess, talked of politics, or just let Henry be Henry in a safe resort. This was the secret between Henry and me and of our marriage. I was his friend, but queen consort to others in the kingdom for the sake of our countries.

Henry's voice brought me back to the present. His voice was authoritative yet soothing when he needed to just be his true self.

"Anne, my queen. You were drifting. The hour is late, but we have a long night ahead of us. Can you give your husband this request?"

I nodded and smiled. "Of course, husband. My apologies. I must have gotten caught up in the moment. Please begin. Say what you need to say. I will listen, always."

"Queen Anne, you know the marriage was only struck to aid my kingdom and your brother's. From that, I know we have shared many nights. Nights between you and me as friends, not husband and wife. You have been agreeable. I feel like finally, we've become friends if nothing more." He sipped more of the red wine, eventually finishing his goblet. I noticed he nodded to my lady, and she began scribing. He stood from the chair and came over to me, putting his hand on my shoulder. I knew this would happen. Henry needed to be Henry. I gave him the comfort of being himself. The curtains darkened the room at night. He opened them to look at the moon and gave a deep sigh.

"I cannot lie to you, Anne. I can lie to many others, but not to you. You have done nothing wrong but be a loving and dutiful, obedient wife, a queen consort to all in the kingdom, and you have never shamed me. In fact, I enjoy the nights we spend together in each other's company, playing, laughing, and drinking. It's almost as if you could remind me of my brother Arthur. God, I miss Arthur so. Our grandmother, rest her soul, wanted me to be raised in the ways of the Church. Arthur was the king. God took my dear brother so early and — well, I thought I would marry Catherine and provide a line of heirs for the sake of the Tudor line. And I was punished.

"And then there was my sweet, sweet Anne. Coy and beautiful, she intoxicated me, but then she plotted behind my back. She was put in the tower and sentenced to death. Ah, my Jane, a true queen, who bore me Edward. A son. An heir that survived and one that you accepted, though he is not yours. Jane even brought my sweet daughters back to me, though they are just girls. She died shortly after Edward's birth but was truly deserving of a queen's funeral.

"Oh Anne, then you came to me, part of an alliance to

be forged, but in the end, instead, a friendship I didn't know I needed. You ask for nothing in return but are always there when I need it most. You know of my decision to reconsider our union. But you do not lose your kindness toward me. How do you do it?"

Looking at Henry, I could sense that he was lost in thought. He was obviously wanting something to come of this evening. I must be patient and let him just speak endlessly if he must. His soul must bear a heavy weight of all the world on his shoulders. Instead of saying something in return, I simply moved to refill his goblet of red wine. I knew Henry, sometimes better than he knew himself.

"Thank you, wife. But as usual, I digress. Anne, my heart and body are calling me to another. You have seen young Catherine, no? I must have her as my wife, but you have given me no offense to divorce you or behead you. I'm not fond of that, but I must have my way. You understand, don't you? A king must honor a marriage alliance when made. You have been a companion and never caused a great offense to me or my kingdom. In fact, you have accepted my heir without shame, knowing he will rule instead of any children that come from your womb. The things we can talk about would make my council truly shudder. Lest they know the influence you have on me, as a confidant."

I thought this was where he wanted me to respond, unlike before. I had to consider this situation. I'd prepared myself for months should this time come to pass, and I was ready. I did not wish to lose my head, but I also did not wish to return to Germany. England was my home now. I looked at my husband. What he spoke was the truth. We were married in name only.

"Henry, dear Henry. Please sit by me, but only so my words can be heard by just you and Lady Mary. You never know about servants. I'm sure I'm just over concerned for your well-being, Majesty. Come, let's play a game of chess, too, while I speak in return. Yes?"

Henry came and sat by me so we could begin a game of chess. This was usually how our conversations went, over a game of chess and wine. Always wine.

"I knew you were not attracted to me since I made my first appearance. I knew what our marriage was. But I think you need a genuine friend, not one with politics on the land or religious agreements in mind. I humbly think you need a friend to let you just be Henry, son of Henry VII and Elizabeth of York. Nothing more, nothing less. You have advisors to the king, Henry, in that respect. But I would like to think we're friends. I will not oppose your desires for Catherine or to even wed her or any other. As for your children and heir, they are your treasures. I merely wish to be of help to them when you are busy with kingdom affairs or if the girls need a mother for certain things. I wish solely for your happiness, and I will not lie to you. I'd like to keep my head, of course, but I would like to be your friend. I think we can be the greatest of friends. What do you propose we do? I will obey your wish and command as my king and husband bids."

I noticed my lady Mary was growing uneasy in case I lost my temper or the king lost his. But I gave her a knowing look, and she calmed down. I breathed deeply and turned to face Henry. When Henry was solemn like he was now, I knew better than to antagonize him. He carried the weight of all of

England on his strong shoulders, despite the growing ulcers in his legs and the constant draining of the puss he had to endure. I didn't want to hurt this great man.

"Henry, tell me your thoughts. What do you want to do? Look for your happiness and think of your people. I am nothing more than your humble servant."

"Oh Anne, I am so grateful that you are this kind and obedient, unlike the other wives. I propose this to you. Agree to an annulment to end this marriage, and I will grant you—I will provide for your life as long as you live, grant you estates to retire in, and a close friendship with me as long as you also remain in England. I don't want to miss our games together or our long talks. I need those with you, Anne. Only you seem to be the one to understand me. What do you say to this?"

"Henry, of course, I agree to remain friends and be your confidant should you need that. I am humbled by your generous offer. I know my appearance makes you compare me to a horse or a jackass, but may I ask a personal request? I am nervous about asking it now with everything being scribed. I would like one more personal thing, but I do not feel right asking."

"Lady Mary, scribe this: I, King Henry VIII, promise to provide Queen Anne her request of any personal nature when she so desires to ask this of me. I will honor my promise to her upon the agreement of an annulment to the marriage, amongst the other things agreed upon already. And Lady Mary, I want two copies of tonight. One for me and one for Anne, so she may know my words are true."

I heard the words and couldn't believe my ears. Henry was the sweetest man, despite his unhealthy ways. I would not have to return to Germany or live as a dowager queen. I could retire comfortably, and the only thing I would lose was my station. And I got to keep my head intact!

"Oh, Lady Mary, please scribe once more this: Upon an agreement for the annulment, Anne of Cleves will now be known as the King's Beloved Sister and treated as if she were part of my birth family, with the same respect as if she were blood to me. She is to be welcomed at court always and have a place near me, for we are kin from the day of the annulment forward. This contract signed by both Henry VIII, King of England, and Queen Anne on this day. And when you have finished this, Lady Mary, see that copies are made for safekeeping because I fear treachery among persons close to my person."

I was honored and moved to hear these words from Henry's own lips. I even wondered what Sir Thomas Cromwell or the others would have to say to such a respected title given to my person. I did not fancy the slightest what Sir Thomas Cromwell would think, considering he was in the Tower for displeasing the king, but he'd helped to forge this alliance. Not to lose favor, I changed the topic, knowing exactly what my husband, or "soon to be brother," needed.

"Henry, I was wondering if we could play another game. Do you still have time this evening? I would like that now that we can be the dearest of friends."

Henry moved his pieces along the board. The games usually lasted long because we were both quite good at the game, and before we knew it, Lady Mary had fallen asleep in the chair, snoring loudly as a boar. Henry and I laughed at both the sight and sound of it. And to think, this was going to be the start of a wonderful friendship that I hoped would last his lifetime and mine.

We spent the rest of the night laughing and playing as good friends do, while my great Lady Mary continued to snore till the morning.

Eventually, Henry bade me good night and made his way to his chambers alone. I spent the rest of the time content in the friendship, the annulment, and the secret wish I would ask of Henry when the time was right. In my heart, I knew this was right for him and for me. I was not the same foolish girl as when I'd first arrived in England months ago.

Chapter One

The Annulment — July 9, 1540
Anne

At the moment my eyes opened to one of the driest mornings England had had recently, I realized the utmost importance of the day. I was content with mind, body, and spirit. My conscience was without guilt or hate. Not only did it feel right, but I couldn't be more eternally happy that I could live and keep my head intact. I knew I kept saying that to myself, but one never knew, the way court could be, if that would be short-lived. But I knew Henry. He would honor his word to me above all else. We had become that close and trusting of one another in the eight months I'd known him. But this was not known to all the courts yet.

One of the younger ladies-in-waiting came running into my room in a daze of confusion. She was breathing hard and was upset by something. Lady Mary took her aside and began speaking to her. I could make out some words, but there must have been gossip in the court about what today was going to be. I was not worried because Henry and I had spent a long night agreeing and becoming better friends. It was probably the best week of the marriage by far, as we were closer to one another than ever before.

"Young lady, stop your fretting, and tell me this instant what is the urgency of having you run into the queen's chambers in such a manner?"

The young girl stopped fidgeting and instead fumbled with her skirts. She didn't want to offend me, but she spoke plainly. "The king…the king is going to cast our queen aside today. I fear we have displeased the king somehow. We will lose our heads."

She cried. I knew I needed to speak to my ladies, and quickly.

I rose from my bed, drawing back the curtains to let the morning light in. Instead of having Lady Mary offer my robe, I simply took the robe off the chair and covered my bodice with it. Lovingly, I pushed a fallen hair from the young girl's face and found my handkerchief to dry her tears. I called all my ladies to gather and listen to what I had to say.

"Ladies. Everything is as it should be. The king and I have made an agreement, one which sees me as his loving sister. We knew the marriage would not last, but a friendship was made, and it would dishearten us both if I did not agree to an annulment. You will serve the next queen, and I will have new ladies to attend to me. And the king will treat us well. We are nothing but his most humble servants. Do you understand?"

The ladies were whispering in disbelief that I would not be beheaded or disgraced. I was their queen, soon to be the King's Beloved Sister and their mistress. They would continue to serve the queen of England. All was as it should be.

"But ladies, for this announcement to be made, we must look the part. I must look the part. Help me bathe and dress. We represent His Majesty in all things and will do as he commands."

A commotion went about in my chambers most of the morning, considering the bathing, dressing, and the questions from my ladies where we would live after today and more. I did my best to maintain composure while offering them all the comfort I could that no one would suffer the same fate that Catherine or Anne had in the past. A lot of these ladies had also been ladies in their households, and they remembered all too well these past wives' fall from grace. But amazingly enough, I had turned a horrific fate into something so much more pleasant.

I had one of my ladies choose a gown to match what Henry would wear today. I learned from his page that Henry would wear his green and gold tunic, and thus, I would wear my green and gold gown to match. We would face the annulment together as man and wife but celebrate with tonight's surprise feast as brother and sister.

As soon as I was made presentable and ready, the king knocked on the door, and a servant opened it widely. King Henry looked in good health, and for the day, a gleam shone in his eyes. His beard was carefully trimmed, and his sword hung by his side. He looked regal. His hand ushered a chamberlain forward, and in his hand was a dark jewel box fastened by a gold "A." The servant opened it, and the king removed the necklace.

"Anne, dearest wife, accept this necklace to wear today to mark the occasion of our new beginning. Are you ready?"

I smiled and thanked him most profusely as he placed the gold necklace around my neck and kissed my cheek. He whispered that all would be done as we had agreed, and he thanked me again and again for being so acquiescent. Holding out his arm, I took it, and my ladies gathered behind us. We made our way to the throne room, which we had decided would be most fitting for the occasion. In fact, Henry and I had spent all week planning the celebration. It was something he decided we would do together to show all of England that he was the king. As servants passed us in the hall, they stopped to bow or curtsy while showing no sign of knowledge that this was all carefully planned. I could hear the whispers amongst the servants, guests, and many others as we made our way into the throne room.

The throne room, carefully designed and beautifully decorated to fit the Tudor name, was immaculate. The king and queen's thrones sat there, empty, waiting for us. Our last act as king and queen consort of England together. After Henry's speech and announcement, we would move to the festivities, including a jousting match to be held in our honor. I knew that part was hard on Henry, as his jousting accident that led to his ulcers and many other sickly ailments still bothered him in his dreams.

As we walked arm in arm toward the thrones, I felt myself remembering coming to court to marry this man, and as my thoughts were carrying me away, a trumpeter sounded our arrival. The audience became silent and unsure of what was happening, considering the gossip that had filled the halls. I had even come to believe part of the gossip was started by none other than Henry himself. We had talked about having fun with this annulment, and in fact, Henry seemed relieved that I was agreeable to such an event. Unbeknownst to him, part of it was that I had no intention of losing my head. I kept reminding myself of that fact and really having no one else in England. As I was a stranger, I would rather be in His Majesty's good graces.

Henry waited till I sat and straightened out my gown. My ladies took their positions throughout to be sure to attend to me with a wave of my hand. He looked at me and smiled. I gave him a slight nod in return and faced the audience. A servant appeared to the king's right and handed him a scroll tied with a ribbon. Henry took the scroll and unraveled it to read it. The look on Henry's face quickly turned sour, and he instantly tore up the annulment parchment. The servant was dumbfounded but stepped back and apologized for offending His Majesty.

"This is not the scroll I was expecting for today. Someone has changed my words to cause me offense. Was it you, or did that traitor Cromwell put you up to this? I smell his hand in this somehow."

The man looked rather uncomfortable, but I remained silent and let Henry take control of the situation. I noticed he was fumbling as if trying to find another scroll like it was an unfortunate accident. I did wave Lady Mary to my side to clean up the mess, but to keep the scroll pieces so we could put together this parchment that displeased my king so. Henry's face was reddening, but then he saw me take control with my lady, and his face softened. Instead of yelling, he extended his hand toward me, which I took and rose from my chair.

"Ladies and gentlemen of the court of England, Queen Anne and I have an announcement, though it seems others have their own announcement to make, which will not happen, I will make ours instead to mark the beginning of the festivities we have lined up for today. Come, Anne, join me at my side." This was my cue to show the court the unity that Henry and I had made.

"Queen Anne has accepted my proposal to an annulment from this day forth. In return, she is to receive all formalities and respect because of her new title as the 'The King's Beloved Sister.' In fact, she is to be honored above all women in England save my wife and daughters. She has shown strength, courage, and honor by agreeing with my request, and I will provide for her till the end of her days." Turning to me, he bowed and said, "Lady Anne, my beloved sister, you are welcome always at my court and my side. Shall you begin the feast, sister?"

I curtsied to my king and, turning to the audience, I curtsied to them as well. "Let's celebrate with a feast. But first, a jousting match in honor of this memorable event. Lady Mary, bring the children to the king, for they will celebrate with us."

The court was mumbling about what they'd just heard. The court gossip must not have prepared them for the reality that was set upon them. For some odd reason, the English court seemed to fancy beheadings and the demise of Henry's wives, except for poor, sweet Jane. No one ever wished for a woman to die from childbirth complications. I watched the men of the court especially. It made me wonder what they were thinking. I was sure it was something like the king must have lost his faculties for a moment to not punish me or divorce me the way he had with the others. I particularly noticed that Henry was not amused in the slightest by certain members of the court, but I remained silent, ever watching. One thing Henry had grown to understand about me was that I could play the part of political manipulation keenly while portraying innocence. In fact, it was my suggestion that we keep the alliance with my brother as long as it was in Henry's favor, not my brother's.

Henry addressed the court once more. "I know Thomas Cromwell has many friends among the court, even after being made known as the treacherous traitor he is. Though he seeks to support the annulment through his letters now, that does not make it true. He is a traitor to the crown and to my person. But there will be no bloodshed this day, save whatever happens on the field during the jousting tournament. Today's festivities are a celebration of kinship between Lady Anne and I."

A man called out, "Long live the king. Long live the king. Long live Lady Anne. Long live Lady Anne."

The court moved to the outside to enjoy the jousting match. In fact, Henry had one of his knights compete in his place. As a moment of honor, he announced to all that the knight would take his place and wear the colors of Lady Anne, his most beloved sister. I was overflowing with emotion at such an honor that I hugged His Majesty, and in return,

Henry embraced me. With a wave, the competition began. The stands were filled with lots of cheering—some booing, but more cheering. Everything was done in fun and jest. It was the most jovial afternoon it could be, despite the intense heat that was not the norm for England.

The last joust was about to begin when I caught Henry looking at the young Catherine Howard. I smiled at seeing how happy Henry was.

"Henry, invite her to sit with us. I will enjoy the last match while you see if Catherine would make you a good wife. She was a wonderful lady in my court, always giggling and making jokes."

Henry looked surprised at my offer but realized the annulment had been accepted and announced, causing no issues with his right to do such a thing. "Oh Anne, sweet sister, I marvel at your grace and kindness. I will ask her to come sit with us. I will come to you later tonight and seek your thoughts if this would be a match for me. Do you mind?"

"Not at all, my lord. I will have a lady fetch us all some wine to enjoy. I would love to get to know Catherine."

As I summoned my lady to prepare refreshments, Catherine sat near Henry and smiled at his flirtations. I nodded to her to take the goblet, and I toasted us all on this most joyous occasion. Then the knight caught my eye, and I turned my attention to finish watching the joust, to give Henry and Catherine a little privacy, but not without being a little curious to sneak a peek at them now and again. The trumpet announced the joust was over, and Henry stood to make the winner known. The knight that wore my colors was the champion of the joust and received not only a purse of gold but a heartfelt handshake and an invitation to dine with us at our table.

The crowds dissipated to the banquet hall. Hampton Court was richly decorated to commemorate this occasion and to let everyone know I was to always be welcomed at court. I retired to my room only to freshen, and as my ladies removed my bodice, a servant entered, carrying a note with the king's seal. Lady Mary, being the most senior, took the note and brought it straight to my hands.

As I opened it, I read the following in Henry's own hand.

You shall find us a perfect friend, content to repute you as our dearest sister. We shall, within five or six days, determine your state, minding to endow you £4000 of yearly revenue. Your loving brother and friend, H.

I gave this dearest note to Lady Mary with the instructions to keep it safe with my other treasures. I wore a red and gold gown in honor of Henry and the Tudor rose. I kept the necklace on for this dinner.

My ladies and I arrived in the banquet room to find a combination of the most delicious dishes the kitchens could muster with our instructions. It included favorite foods of Henry's and mine, as well as dishes from both England and Germany. We celebrated the alliance with this annulment to show the court that Henry was strong and virile in his appetites. Servants lined the walls with the plates of food, waiting to serve once we were sitting. Henry saw me enter and immediately moved to escort me. I was to sit next to him as if I were still queen for this night.

The music filled the halls, and the dancing was

marvelous. Henry ate sparingly as if something were troubling him, but his eyes remained fixated on Catherine. I took no notice of my plate until Lady Mary nudged me as if begging me to eat. I took a small bite of the quail, and it was succulent as ever.

"My lord, you seem troubled during this banquet. What ails your mind at this moment?" I smiled at him, waiting for him to either respond or not.

"Ah, Anne. I do fancy Catherine. Did you get my personal note? I am going to give you the most wonderful estates unless you have a favorite. I hate to see you go to another estate, but that just means I will have to visit you often, sister."

I giggled and loved him for his generosity. "Will you dance with me, dear brother?" It seems we had taken to our new titles with great affection.

Henry led me to the floor, and the music filled the room. We danced and danced, laughing while doing so. Suddenly, we came right next to Catherine. She was a young girl and obviously shy, but she knew she caught the king's eye. I extended one hand to her while the other held Henry's.

"Sweet Catherine. Will you do us the honor of dancing with us?" I asked her nicely and sweetly so as not to make her uncomfortable.

"Yes, my lady," she said with a curtsy.

After a few turns, I whispered to Henry that I must go get a glass of wine, as I was getting a little dizzy. I told them both that they were in excellent hands with each other. With that, I returned to my seat and took the glass of wine that Lady Mary handed to me and raised it to them as they looked my way. I was happy for Henry to see him alive once again, and secretly, I hoped this would be one match that would last and provide him with the male heirs he wanted.

Toward the end of the banquet, Henry and I stood together, proclaiming the annulment was not just an end to the marriage but a beginning of a kinship we both held dear. We thanked our guests and eventually retired to my chambers for a few rounds of chess and wine, as well as my approval of Lady Catherine.

Chapter Two

Thoughts of the Heart — May 1541
Henry

My leg's ulcer leaked the pungent puss once more, and I took my leave of her in the middle of our intimacy. As much as her body made me feel young again, I grew weary of her childish behavior. Sometimes I wondered if she had any sense of how to behave like a queen. Maybe I was getting too old for the young and pretty things, but seven simple years lay between her and my daughter Mary. And Mary, I must admit, behaved so much like her mother. A true queen in her own presence. Dead these last few years, and still the people rejoiced in her name: Katherine of Aragon. I knew I had loved her in the beginning, but every male son would not survive. Only Mary. Sometimes I wondered if marrying Katherine was punishment from the almighty Lord.

I entered the king's chambers and commanded all to

leave but two of my servants. Thomas Culpepper had a talent to make the poultice strong enough but without such a strong odor that I may pass out. I sent the other servant to fetch me Lord Charles Brandon. I knew I was in one of my moods, and somehow, only Lord Brandon was worthy of my innermost trust. My mind was wandering until the poultice, barely touching my ulcer, brought me back to my senses. Grabbing for a sheet, I clenched my teeth in pain until Lord Brandon appeared. He looked worse for the wear, but he reassured me he was not ill, just tired. We were all tired. Peace reigned, at least for a little time. But inside, my heart yearned for action. It just seemed my body did not wish to partake.

Charles took over for Thomas Culpepper and gave him a knowing look. The young lad took his leave, and Charles and I were left in the privacy of my chambers. As my leg endured the poultice, Charles knelt beside the bed. I could see he was tired and did not move as swiftly as we once did when we were sturdy lads. But I never had a more trustworthy ally and confidant. I could bare my secrets to him, and I knew they would never leave his lips. He carried out my most hard orders, and yet, despite his secret marriage to my sister without my consent as his king, I could not find fault with him. But I knew he had to be punished. So, the fine was issued, but that never stopped my brotherly love for him nor his for me. I touched his shoulder as if to show him the brotherly affection that stood between us.

"Henry, what is it? You have need of me?"

"How long have we been friends now, Charles? A long time, I should think. It's almost as if we are brothers. Catherine is beautiful, is she not? But somehow, I miss the grace of Lady Anne of Cleves in the court. I don't know why I am a cursed man. Different queens should produce heirs to the throne, but alas, I have only one. My sweet Edward. Anne knew her place and her duty, but I did not like her before. Yet somehow, I want to visit her. But Catherine cannot know of this. She is young, and I am hopeful she will bear me many sons. Though her simplicity annoys me. I don't know why, but she is so childlike. Maybe we show our age, eh?"

Charles nodded and stood to return the poultice to the table of medicines. He looked about the room to ensure none of the servants had quietly entered without us knowing. Straightening his tunic, he asked for my permission to speak freely. It was given.

"Henry, it's the irony of age and of God, I think. At times, he grants us his divine mercy where we live in peace, with heirs, beautiful wives, and in love. Then, to show us his power, he takes one of those things that we hold dear away from us. Henry, what do you need me to do this time? Do you have a need for a mistress? Is Catherine not doing her duty? Tell me, Henry, what it is you need. I know not a lot about medicines for your leg, but I will do my best to rid that pain for you somehow. But I'm not too well prepared should you send me out for a battle." He chuckled at his comment, hoping to make me smile.

He did. I simply laughed. My mind wandered again, lost in my thoughts. I saw Charles sit and wait for me to respond. I let my mind wander a bit so then I could give Charles a response to be carried out.

I thought fondly of Arthur, my brother. He was young when God took him from us. The rightful king of England as my father's first son. Then, I thought of all my sons I had lost over the years. To God. I was God's holy servant in all this, and yet he punished me. Why? Perhaps it was true, I should never have married Katherine of Aragon, but I divorced her to cleanse my soul. Would Arthur and Katherine have had many sons? Would my life have been found in the Church somehow? Maybe there would never have been a separation, and we would still be Catholics.

Coming back to face Charles, I looked as regal as I could despite the pain in my leg.

"Charles, I am sending you on a special mission. Take Mary and Elizabeth with you. It's not a mission of politics, but I want you to inquire about Lady Anne of Cleves. Bringing my daughters to visit with her will let her know I am true to my word. She is the king's sister, after all. Check on her well-being and see if our friendship holds true. I think it does, but I want to be sure. Let the girls spend a little time with her. It might do them all good while I attend to Catherine and try to get an heir from her. Then, report back to me when you restore her health and well-being. Do this for me, Charles. I want…I want to know she is happy and whatever else she may share with you."

Charles looked at me with those questioning eyes, and I turned my attention to my leg. I did not want to share my thoughts just yet until I knew what news he brought me of Lady Anne. Realizing that I had not told him when to leave, I explained he must leave before the end of the week, allowing the girls and their ladies to prepare for departure. I bade Charles to fetch us ale and to take a seat. I had more to discuss with him.

Taking a large drink of ale, I then placed the goblet on the table. I reached for my cane to help me out of bed and called for Culpepper. "Dress me, boy. Do it fast. Lord Brandon and I are hungry. Go seek something from the kitchens after you dress me."

Breads, meats, and cheeses were later brought, and again, we drank and began contemplating. Charles was a dear friend whose loyalty and opinion I could trust. I beseeched him once more to explore how to please the almighty God so he would not take his dissatisfaction out on me once more. Charles knew just how. I liked his idea and made it so. Effective immediately, every church in England would hold its own copy of the Great Bible in English so everyone could read the word of God and know the proper behavior in serving God. Perhaps, as I told Charles, this might grant favor with God in giving me a son that would live. It was too much burden on my only son in case God sought to punish me again.

Charles, also lost in thought because of my many questions, shared a personal secret with me. "Majesty, do you miss her, your sister Mary, as much as I do? I know we offended you years ago, and we repaid the debt to Your Majesty's treasure, but sometimes I miss the way she liked to play cards or test my perseverance in things. But if I misspeak, Majesty, tell me, and I will not do so again."

"Yes, I miss her. But I swear to you, Mary was always a spirit that could not be controlled. You know that. She reminded me of my mother, Queen Elizabeth of York. She could be both proper and spirited in the way she loved my father. Charles, go to my Lady Anne. I want you to give her a brotherly token of my loyalty and thankfulness for her agreement."

I handed him a locket fit for a queen. I saw Charles look at it, and he recognized it. A tear fell from his eyes.

"Tell you what, Charles. Swap that locket out for this one. Give this one to Lady Anne. The one that made that tear, keep it. I forgot how it was Mary's, given to her by my mother. Keep this as a remembrance on those lonely days when you miss her." I could tell he was moved as I closed his fist around the locket that once belonged to his love.

Charles bowed and made haste for his trip with the ladies, Mary and Elizabeth. I found myself alone in my room, cradling my leg until my men in the chamber came to me with urgent news. Apparently, Queen Catherine required my attention, but I refused to see her in my current state. I knew I had left her abruptly because of this cursed leg of mine. Instead, I had Culpepper find Master Holbein and encouraged him to give her art lessons or something. This should amuse her for some time—at least, I hoped.

Taking to my bed, I ordered for the cardinal. Being king did not end, despite my leg's constant pain. While I waited for the cardinal, my mind slipped away from me again, this time to my Lady Mother. She was a good queen and a loving mother and had loved my father like no other. If only I could find a queen like her and her mother before her, who was famous for bearing heirs. Maybe I needed a distraction that would call my queen to bear an heir. Catherine had been my wife for over six months now, and I had bedded her more often than I realized, and still, her womb was as empty as a hollow log. Just the thought of it made me boil with anger, but I knew I must get my heir through her somehow. She was young. I grew weary of the fruitless task even though I enjoyed the act, but I wanted to see victory in the deed.

As I lay thinking about Catherine's sweet body, my manhood came alive. Though I would not publicly admit that it failed me, somehow, the thought of Catherine made it rise to the occasion. Again my mind lay wandering on so many thoughts. Perhaps my Lady Grandmother was right in having me educated so much in various subjects that I could find myself not just wise in the wisdom of religion but in words and history. Perhaps I needed a battle or a war to spur me on further than just surrounding myself with useless servants. But Lady Anne. So good and obedient as a wife should be, similar and yet different from Jane. Both were good wives, and yet I was with Catherine now, my young lustful wife.

The cardinal finally heeded my call and bowed mercifully. I rose from my bed as best I could and prepared my presentation before him. I looked upon his red robes and the Holy Cross that he symbolically wore around his papal neck, presenting my ring for His Grace to kiss.

"Majesty."

"Cardinal, I request you to check on my son Edward's care regarding his faith. He spends far too much time with some who are supposedly aligned with, let's say, other matters. I don't want his mind exploited, except for which I have ordered. Also, check on His Highness's level of care in the nursery. In three years, he should begin his formal education, and I am charging you to find a suitable tutor to present to me for consideration. Also, make sure every precaution and level of cleanliness meets the young heir. For one day, he will need to be healthy as a horse to bring more heirs to the throne. You may go now."

"Your Majesty, there is another matter I wish to discuss with you. It concerns the queen."

Not again. I did not want to hear anything about the queen while my leg festered in this disgusting, putrid puss.

The cardinal left as I had waved my hand in dismissal. I had no patience today to listen to the tales of the court, except for what Charles came back to me with. I must have news of the Lady Anne. I didn't know why, but I felt as if part of me missed playing cards and other vices with her.

"Culpepper, come here, boy."

Culpepper, always standing at the ready near me, rushed over and looked at me, waiting for an order. What a simple mind, but he came from an excellent family. In fact, his brother was a knight. And he, a loyal servant, trusting enough to be in my privy chamber.

"I want you to teach the queen some of the card games. I will play with her once she learns. Until then, tell her I hope she is well and in good health. I shall visit her soon."

Alone with my thoughts again, I let myself think once more of Lady Anne before retiring. My leg burned, waking me from my slumber. My hand clenched the sheet, and the boy sent for my physician. Bustling about in my rooms made me fully awake, and as I looked at my leg, I could see the blisters forming, blood spilling from the wounds. God was continuing to punish me, his faithful servant.

My physician made a stronger poultice and placed it on my thigh. This time I felt it more than ever, and I bit into a piece of leather. The poultice sent a burning sensation into my thigh, and I was sure my blood could feel it working its wonders. Not knowing what to do, the physician sought my consent to administer another poultice on top of this one simultaneously so that once the treatment was over, I might sleep. I nodded and closed my eyes as the poultice once more touched my flesh in a more excruciating experience than the first.

Once the treatment was done, the physicians left my chambers, leaving me alone. I dismissed everyone else, except for one servant who delivered a personal note from the queen. He mentioned that Lady Rochester had scribed it for her. I took it and sent him on his way. Opening the note, I read it carefully.

My dearest Henry. I do not know what I did to offend you, but I should like very much to embrace your affections. Will you come to me soon? Thank you for sending Master Culpepper to me to learn cards, but I would rather have your instruction with rewards.

Oh, sweet wife. She taunted me with the underlined words. My manhood rose to the occasion, but I knew I could not perform any acts while my legs were in pain. But once I was well, I knew I would ride my little filly till she bore me an heir! I settled back in bed, hoping to return to slumber, and perhaps by the end of the week, when Charles had left for Lady Anne, I would ride Catherine and beget an heir.

Chapter Three

My First Guests at Hever Castle—May 1541
Anne

A messenger brought me a letter from Lord Brandon, announcing his upcoming visit with the ladies, Mary and Elizabeth. As I read the letter in its entirety, the kind man did not wish to impose on his visit, but he came at the king's request to check on my status and see how things fared now that the summer had begun. He wished to inform me that meats and cheeses were on their way, so their stay did not take away from our food stores. I held the letter close to my breast, thinking fondly of how nice Lord Brandon was when he first met me in the home of my brother, Duke Wilhelm of Cleves. I called for my ladies-in-waiting to hear the news.

My newest lady, Lady Katharine Basset, had become one of my more senior ladies-in-waiting. I gave her charge to teach some of the younger ladies how to serve in case she wished to return to her husband. But she continued to refuse, to make sure first that I had enough friends, as I was still relatively a foreigner. I was happy that both Wymond Carew and his wife could stay in my household while I continued to learn the language.

"Ladies, Lord Charles Brandon is coming, and he is bringing both Lady Mary and Lady Elizabeth. We must make their rooms ready, especially for the young ladies. I'm sure Lord Brandon will be fit in his room. Let's make haste. I think they have already departed, and food shall arrive prior to their arrival. Lady Katharine, come with me."

I had thought of Lady Mary as one of my dearest friends. We were close in age, and I knew from others that she resembled her late mother, Katherine of Aragon. I loved getting to know the young Elizabeth. Mary was much older and already a young woman in her own right. Getting to know Elizabeth was going to be so much fun, and perhaps Lord Brandon would stay long enough to play cards with me again.

We were looking at one room we would provide for Lady Mary. Everything was cheerful, proper, and what a young lady would like after her travels. I knew this would be a difficult time for her, as I had heard that Henry had his daughter's old governess executed on the grounds of being a Catholic. This poor woman had meant a lot to Lady Mary, and I worried how sad she would be. Lady Jane arranged the closet to ensure there was enough room for gowns and other things a young lady would need. And we placed a bible of her faith near her bed, so she may read and pray to God as she saw fit.

As for Lady Elizabeth's rooms, I asked Lady Katharine to ensure that there were things a child still wanted to have, such as dolls and other little girl things, but not to over-do it, as I knew Henry would want her to be treated as a young lady of her stature. After all, Lady Elizabeth was just a tad shy of her ninth birthday. Lady Katharine nodded in acknowledgment, and we went to seek what would be Lord Brandon's rooms. I found a suitable room that I believed gave him privacy and quiet, so he might relax before returning to court.

As we prepared the kitchen staff for additional food and guests coming as representatives of King Henry, there was a knock on the door. Sure enough, it was the food delivery, but much more than cheeses and meats. It was many delicious goods that I let one of my ladies take charge of while I retired to the sitting room to continue to play on the organ. I had learned a little of the history of Hever Castle from them and took pleasure in exploring the rooms and the grounds that once belonged to the Boleyn family. The wood frame that held the house together was strong, but it seemed there had been some work done on it between their owning of it and mine. Then I learned why. Henry had anything, and everything that bore the mark of Boleyn replaced with a Tudor mark. The only jewel I could see he loved that bore any connection to the Boleyn family was Elizabeth. A beautiful girl and I couldn't wait to see her again. And Mary.

I approached the other ladies-in-waiting and urged them to make ready the castle. They were all bustling about like several bees to a rose while I played music to fill the air with harmony. I had hired a music teacher when we left court after Henry's wedding so I could learn to play. In fact, because

I agreed to the annulment, I was living a rather contented life and saw no need for a husband. I enjoyed learning new things and, of course, gambling. In fact, I had held card parties consistently. It became something of an amusement to Lady Katharine, Lady Jane, Lady Mary, and I. Some of my other ladies were not fond of our entertainment. We had enjoyed living at Hever Castle, but we did plan on visiting the other estates Henry had given to me as well. Sometimes, in fact, I forgot Mary was one of my ladies, as I treated her as a friend, which was preferable.

Days were filled with picking flowers to arrange in the rooms for the girls, bringing a delightful smell to freshen them up. A delivery boy arrived in two days with dolls, tiny cups and saucers, and games from the toymaker in town. I wanted Elizabeth to not only be a lady, as she was but still to have a childhood. This would be a visit to her genuine family's home. The poor girl had been raised all over the place, with no place in line to the throne. Perhaps Henry would change his mind one day, the same for Mary. Both girls were a joy to their father in their own way.

Roaming the garden grounds gave me a sense of peace, at least until Lady Mary came running toward me with a letter from my brother.

I read the letter quietly at first, and then translated it into English. Though my English was still not as nice sounding as Lady Mary's, I managed it. He wrote of our mother, who missed me terribly, and that if I should want to return, I could. But I did not. I'd rather enjoy being in England, where I could learn to read and write English, play the organ and other musical instruments, and gamble. I folded the letter and placed it in a compartment sewn into my gown. I reached for Lady Mary's arm so I could offer her assurance that I would not leave England and for company as I continued to stroll the gardens.

"Mistress Anne, the kitchen wants to know if you prefer a light supper when they arrive or a feast? Everything else has been made ready. And the music teacher has agreed to perform for that evening's entertainment. I even informed the village elders that the game of cards might be postponed because of their arrival."

I thought about that for a moment. I told her to schedule the game of cards for the following night, as Lord Brandon might enjoy that while the girls learned to play. I had hoped that Henry would not mind his daughters learning a game or two.

"We shall have a light supper, as I am sure they might be tired and wish to rest. But have the kitchens prepared for anything."

Lady Mary curtsied and hoisted up her skirts and hastened back to the kitchens while I continued to walk and think about what the reason could be for Henry to send visitors. Was he ill? Was Catherine? Ever since last July, Henry had written me letters, albeit brief letters, but letters. He talked of his happiness but always inquired after me. I told no one of these letters, not even Lady Mary. In fact, it was always delivered through a messenger from either someone the king trusted or someone from Lord Brandon's service.

A boy came running toward me, completely out of breath.

"Mistress! Mistress! Wait a minute, I need to catch my

breath."

I laughed at the boy's excitement and urged him to breathe slowly. Finally, he told me that Lord Brandon and the princesses had arrived, and they wanted him to fetch me. I gave him my thanks and a coin for his speed.

"You earned this coin for your quick feet. Save this in your purse, boy."

I made my way back to the castle and found Lady Elizabeth waiting for me in the chair closest to the organ. Her beautiful reddish hair reached past her shoulders, and she ran to me. Looking at her rosy cheeks, I smiled at her. She looked so much like Henry.

"Where is Lady Mary? And Lord Brandon? Or did you come here all by yourself, Lady Elizabeth?"

She giggled and gave me that sheepish smile that showed her dimples. Then I saw Lady Mary enter and curtsy. She was a beautiful young woman and would make any man happy to have her. If only Henry could see that. I returned the curtsy to her and welcomed her with open arms.

"Lady Anne, it is so good to see you. How are you liking it here? I'm so glad you are still in England."

"Lady Mary, it is a joy to see you and the Lady Elizabeth. Do you know how long I shall have to enjoy this visit with you both? I would like so much to spend as much time as I can with you girls. I hope you feel the same in return."

Lady Elizabeth just giggled away. "Can I tell her, Mary? Can I please?"

Lady Mary nodded.

"Father, the king, said we can stay as long as we would like but to return before summer is over. We are going to have so much fun together! But Lord Brandon can't stay that long. He has to return to the king after he visits with you."

"Well then, we must not make any delay. We can't have the king upset by anything. Where is Lord Brandon?"

I looked through the estate for Lord Brandon and found him talking to my ladies. I glanced about and saw how taken they were with him. He looked a little older than when I'd first met him, his hair grayer and his eyes more solemn. I recalled how he would talk fondly of his one wife, Henry's sister, Mary. He'd felt more alive with her than any other woman at court. He didn't hear me come in, as I wanted him to rest and recoup before supper. One of my ladies saw me approach and announced my entrance. He immediately stood and waited for me to extend my hand. As I did, he bowed and kissed my hand ever so lightly.

"Lady Anne, how do you fare here in Hever Castle? Are you well enough?"

"I am, Lord Brandon. I'm as content as I ever have been. His Majesty was gracious to give me this estate, and I have grown to love it here, but I also love being at Richmond. How was the journey?"

Lord Brandon coughed a little and asked if we could talk somewhere privately. Obediently, my ladies all left to attend to the ladies Mary and Elizabeth. I ushered him to sit while I poured him a bit of ale. He seemed wary, but he retrieved from his pocket a small bundle, wrapped in a beautiful cloth with a charm attached to it, holding the letter "A."

"This is from the king, Your Grace. He hopes you are well and finding your way among our culture, as well as your happiness."

I quickly opened the little bundle and found the most beautiful set of charms and a matching locket. The locket, once I opened it, carried a picture of Henry and Edward on one side, and the ladies Mary and Elizabeth on the other. I clutched this treasure to my breast and gave him a heartfelt smile. Such an age difference between us, but he had always been kind to me. I could tell he must have things on his mind. He was so much like Henry that I knew to wait for when he was ready to speak about what troubled him. Surely the king couldn't be displeased with me or my ladies. Not only did I ensure that Lord Brandon had a full cup of ale, but I excused myself to seek refreshments from the kitchen.

I knew I would be scolded for not using my ladies or other servants in my household, but this newfound freedom was something to be enjoyed. No lady could gamble the way I did, live freely without a husband, and own several estates and be taken care of by the king himself. If I returned to my brother, I would forsake the life Henry had given to me, and as I thought of him fondly while carrying the refreshment tray, I realized how lucky I was compared to the other queens in Henry's life. I remembered Lord Brandon's favorites: extra slices of meat, quail eggs, and cheese, and the cook had included fresh apples.

Lord Brandon did not need time to prepare himself to speak. He must have been practicing this entire journey to see how I would respond.

"Lady Anne, I must be frank with you. When Henry sent us here, his desire was more of a personal nature to check on your person and well-being. He wishes to have me verify you are still his most loyal servant and that nothing is amiss. Do you recall how I taught you a few things about cards to help you please His Majesty and to fit in at court? Let's play a game."

I brought out a game table and playing cards. We played with him dealing the cards.

"Henry's leg has been inflamed once more, and when that happens, he becomes very somber and lost in thought. No matter how the sweet young Catherine tempts to ease his suffering, he does not go to her. Instead, secretly, he meets with me, and we reminisce about our past and how we became the men we are today. We fought in one of the first battles when Henry took the throne, and we shared a lot. But he has tasked me to deliver another item of affection to you. Take this and read it when you are able. Then, before I leave, I must have your answer. But aside from this, take heart. Lady Anne, we knew Henry was not used to a queen like you, but Thomas Cromwell, God rest his soul, sought a marriage that would help the reformation and expected Henry to be amenable without question. But what we didn't realize was that Henry was on a personal mission to seek heirs to the throne. A king can't have just one son. Because of your composure, considering the annulment, Henry has been developing a rather keen fondness for Your Grace. But what he asks of you must never be made known to any person save me, you, and His Royal Majesty. Your own ladies must never know this. He wishes to visit you from time to time in secret." He ate and drink and played a couple of hands.

As I listened, I realized that I clearly may not fully understand all the English language yet, but I didn't want to say anything misunderstanding. Was Henry asking me to be a secret mistress? My heart secretly longed for Henry to have affection toward me when we were married, but it wasn't so. I took my letter and opened it, reading every word from Henry carefully. While I read, I knew Lord Brandon was eating and drinking ale. In my thoughts, I forgot about supper or the girls because Henry wrote the words that must never be known to others.

Dearest Anne,

Forgive my hastiness in sending Lord Charles Brandon and Ladies Mary and Elizabeth to you, but I felt it would be less conspicuous should he escort my daughters for a visit with you. The truth is, dearest Anne, I fear I misjudged our marriage without a second thought. I miss the nights we would just talk before sleeping and seeing you when we woke, but the alliance was of great importance. Yes, Queen Catherine will spite me, but the place you have in my heart remains empty. I know you wish to ask me something that you could not speak of before. Therefore, I will come to you personally and secretly so that you may ask of me your secret desire.

Progress has made me itch for some useful purpose in life. Oh, Anne, my heart needs game, my soul needs a bite. I feel I can be me when we talk, just like I can be when I talk to Charles.

I hold you above all except for the queen and my daughters, but I ask of you to love me as your humble servant, Henry.

I folded the letter and returned it to Lord Brandon, telling him he should dispose of this letter, but he refused. Henry wanted me to keep the letter, to remind me of his love and devotion. I would have to secure it somewhere safe. I had my answer, as it was right on the top of my tongue, but I had to ask him if Henry wanted me to write a response or if Charles was to be the messenger. A good faithful servant he was to His Majesty. I knew deep down that to be his mistress would be a detriment, and I was fond of Catherine. She brought life to him where others could not. Could it be because she was only around eighteen years of age?

I motioned for Lord Brandon to play more, hoping that he appreciated the distraction. We must have lost track of time because it was one of my ladies that interrupted us, calling us for the evening meal. Everyone was gathered around, waiting for us to sit.

Elizabeth broke the silence. "Lady Anne, do your ladies sit here too and eat with us?"

To her delight, I replied, "Yes. In my home, we all eat together. We are not as formal as we should be if we were in court. Here, we eat together. Sometimes I even help with the chores while they help me with learning music. I much rather like it this way. Do you?"

Elizabeth giggled and replied with an excited nod of her head. The entire table laughed and told stories as we ate our supper. It was even delightful to see Lady Mary laugh. But I wished for her to have a suiter so much. She deserved one, one that would love her for her. As we ate, I couldn't help but think of Henry's very personal letter. But that secret smile I kept hidden, sure that I would be true to Henry's request.

Mary put her fork down and politely asked, "Ma'am, how shall we pass the time on our visit to you? I am not entirely fond of this castle, for its history may hold some pain for me, but I know Elizabeth might find it of interest. Shall we be doing anything fun?"

My ladies and I had given it much thought prior to their arrival, and we had actually prepared a small game that the entire party would enjoy. My newest lady-in-waiting, Eleanor, took that request and excused herself from the table. She went to fetch a box that we had lovingly prepared and handed it to me. I opened the box and explained to all that we had prepared a fun game that would take Mary and Elizabeth through the house and the gardens to find secret treasures that were listed on these little pieces of parchment paper.

"Oh, Mary, this sounds like fun. It would be joyous to play, don't you think?"

The rest of the evening was spent playing until it was time to retire.

Chapter Four

Betrayal — November 1541
Henry

Thomas Cranmer insisted on my audience to discuss the various complaints and accusations against my wife once again. I loathed him for bringing this to me, but at least he was honest in bringing these transgressions against Catherine. Deep down, I wasn't sure whom to believe anymore. It was driving me insane. I couldn't be a mad king! I couldn't blame Charles for finding her, as she brought me out of my despair, but there was no conceivable reason she hadn't done what I commanded — to bear me a male heir.

"Your Grace, more people of the court continue to witness her behavior, and Your Grace must act. How shall I carry out your command, Majesty?"

Oh God, my mind had been on nothing else but the message that Charles had brought me back from Hever Castle many months ago. My daughters had returned to court, all elated with their time spent there. In fact, Elizabeth continued to ask to return more often. How I would like to visit Hever Castle! I must have been lost in thought because I did not hear Cranmer speak. He cleared his throat.

"Your Majesty? Is it your leg again? I was saying—"

"Archbishop, I have no time for this. Just question her and do it quickly. Lock her in her apartments. Tell me if I need a new wife or not. She's been without my heir for too long. Wretched woman! Leave and fetch Lord Brandon. But do your duty, Archbishop Cranmer."

While I waited for Charles to enter, I pulled out the latest letter my trusted messenger had sent me from Anne. Who would've thought that after all this, I could've had her in my favor? I remembered when Anne Boleyn would write to me, but this was different. This Anne was more intriguing to me, but I did not admit that to anyone but Charles. She was innocent, sweet, and gentle. In fact, I was not ignorant of the fact that people in my court missed her and heard how good she was to my daughters. Opening the letter, I read her words, but I knew them by heart already.

Your Most Gracious Majesty and my Honorable Brother,

I greet you with the sincerest thoughts that your person is well and happy. I must thank you for your special gift. I keep the locket closest to me and hope that one day, you will visit me and I can enjoy playing cards with you again. I hope you remember that promise you made to me what feels like a lifetime ago, yet it has only been one year.

Your Loving Sister and Humble Servant,

Anne of Cleves

A page announced the entrance of Charles, and I turned to face him. He seemed joyous with the peace in the kingdom, much more so now that I had been made King of Ireland. I thought the only battle we grew weary of was that of the Catholics and the pope. I embraced Charles and had him tell me news of Hever Castle or Richmond. He would know that as a sign to make sure all was private between us. My servants left us to our own devices, and I found solace in my thoughts and interests.

"Charles, I must ask your privacy for what I am to confess. Do you give me your word, brother?"

"Yes, Majesty…Henry, of course, I do. As you said, we are brothers."

I sighed and faced Charles. Though I wanted to tell him something deeper about Lady Anne, I began with my confession, something I could not share with the archbishop or anyone in the church. I could feel my heart beating faster and my pulse racing somehow, but at least my leg remained quiet and still. I took a deep breath and removed my hat. Running my hand through my hair, I took the chair nearest to me.

"Charles, I fear that all my marriages have been invalid. I mentioned this once before to Thomas More, but he easily dismissed it without another word. He told me not to worry, but I couldn't get my complete piece out. To all the court, I must govern the land by the laws set forth. I must have an heir. I must rule as true and just. Katherine, the first of my wives—I think I must have been cursed for committing that sin of marrying my brother's widow. Only Mary survived. But I don't want to think about that anymore. I must see Anne, but something in my being is stirring. God, Charles, our bodies fail us, but our hearts have courage, man. The realm is peaceful, and my body longs for war. I need a battle. I'm still a soldier at heart. A soldier who yearns for battle. Do you agree?"

I glanced at Charles and knew the look he had — I was right. We needed action. Damn horse costed me my future in jousting, but I couldn't blame the animal for my accident.

While Charles seemed to contemplate my thoughts, one minister stormed into the room.

"Your Grace, you must come. Lord Brandon, too. There is unrest in one town. The people are fighting over the taxes you sanctioned, and the remaining monasteries are being dissolved. There is civil unrest in various regions of the realm. Might I suggest Your Majesty consider a peaceful progress, or shall we send in Your Majesty's troops?" asked the minister.

"Come, Lord Brandon. It seems we are being summoned. Apparently, my ministers can't function without me." I knew what I said was probably harsh, but I didn't care in the slightest. After all, I was the king.

We tried to move as fast as my leg would allow us, but the movement only made the pain come to life. Halfway down the hallway, I had to stop and call for Thomas Culpepper. "Bring me to my rooms, now. I will not have the court see me this way." Looking at my minister, I said, "Send forth Thomas Cranmer to my rooms as well, forthwith."

As Culpepper and other servants helped me to my rooms, they gave me little privacy as Culpepper helped me to my bed. As chief groom of the body, only he could assist me in such a manner. He prepared a poultice, but one look at the puss leaking from the wound told me that a poultice would not suffice.

"Charles, get my physicians, and I don't care what they are doing or if they are an inconvenience. Bring them to me now, I tell you!"

I fell back against the pillows, and it felt like I was drowning. I grabbed one of the silk pillows and threw them at one of the lowly servants. "Bring me ale. God has cursed me and my leg. Fetch me my ministers and bring me the soldier — What's his name? Sir Peter Carew. I think he should be well rested by now."

As I made my commands known, I could feel the puss burning more than it ever had before. Culpepper placed the poultice more firmly than before on my leg and informed me he used my concoction but doubled the ingredients, knowing that this time the pain was more intense. He was a faithful lad, always eager to please. He should be rewarded somehow, perhaps a pretty wife. Only Culpepper and I knew that the one ingredient that always worked for my leg was worms. Medicine was always a great interest of mine, much to my lady grandmother's dismay. She would've preferred that I stayed faithful to the Catholic Church, I was sure. But I knew my true calling.

As the poultice worked its magic, I was passing in and out of lucidity. What brought me back to my consciousness was the people I demanded to see, all huddled in a circle around me. Matters of State and my person required my immediate attention. I could see the looks of fear on their faces, thinking this was the end. But far from it. All at once they inquired about the state of the realm and what to do, for the heir to the crown was not old enough.

"Fools. I am not dying. You all act like I am dying. I should have your heads for such disloyalty." As I shouted this to them, I threw the goblet nearest to me at them. "Sir Carew, where are you, good sir?"

The soldier, young and solid, approached as if he were ready for a sudden attack or military mission. He had a look of intelligence about him and an awareness that would draw anyone to follow his command.

"Sir Carew, I want you to gather your men and go into one village and inquire as to the rumblings I am hearing about. I want to convey to my good people of England that there are peaceful and joyous times ahead. Bring my Lord Great Chamberlain Radcliffe with you. Might do him some good to get out and about. I am feeling rather generous right now, considering the pain my leg is in."

With all these people mucking about my affairs, sometimes I deeply wished that my brother were king and not I. I was not born for all this frill and fluff. Deep down, my father was always right. Be gentle and kind, but do not forget to show them who is the rightful king to hold the throne, the one that was given greatness by the Lord himself.

The pain subsided for a bit, thanks to this stronger poultice Culpepper had made. Thomas Cranmer made his way to my line of sight.

"Your Majesty, I must clarify your point from earlier order. Shall I begin at once or be patient awhile? While you may not die today, Your Majesty still needs another heir to the throne. This is of great importance, especially if the rumors are true."

"Fool. I know that. Tell the queen that she is not to leave her apartments, and release most of her ladies. Leave but one or two to provide comfort, but only that. But, for the love of God, do not tell her of my well-being, no matter how much she begs or asks. Let her answer the interrogatories first. Then, Sir Brandon and I are going on a pilgrimage to Hever Castle. I am in the mood for a card game there. Charles, make the arrangements for me. The rest of you, leave now. Do not question my person again!"

Everyone left rather quickly, and Culpepper used his position as my Gentleman of the Privy Chamber to speak to me in a manner that would not be tolerated by me otherwise. As my gentleman, he reminded me that often, my mood went from sour to miserable rather quickly when my leg was in pain. He suggested perhaps I shouldn't let my council, archbishops, or anyone else in my rooms except for him and Charles. I didn't like his tone, and I snapped at him, nearly taking his head with my words, but I knew he was right. He didn't flinch once at my words, but he prepared more of the poultice that only he and I knew what was in it. It was more than normal, but this time, I felt my legs were not as strong as they once were. The physicians wanted to bleed me, but Culpepper said he would manage it.

While another round of poultice was taking effect, Culpepper knew what to do. He suggested I consider the point that Cranmer kept insisting about. Another thing he asked was if there was no other heir, perhaps I should consider another worthy to be queen, but only if Catherine would step aside. Another annulment? But with the rumors I had been informed of, I was not sure an annulment would be entertained by Catherine. I had to decide what to do with the queen if she was truly guilty of the things being rumored of her past. But who would be worthy of me, Henry VIII, King of England?

Culpepper looked sheepishly at my leg and then at me. It was as if he wished to say something but didn't.

"Speak, boy. What is on your mind?"

Culpepper didn't respond at first as he glanced around the room, being ever so vigilant. "Your Majesty, it is not I to question your orders, but I beseech you if you really thought about what happens if the queen admits to her past. What will you do then?"

I hadn't thought about it, but I assumed because it was a crime against our marriage, my sweet Catherine would have to lose her head at some point. Then my mood became sour. I guessed I would have to send my men back to the drawing board to find me another new wife. But a wife that would bear my sons!

As I felt my mood change, Culpepper could remedy my leg again. I was up and about again, ready to tackle my kingdom's problem.

"Leave me, boy. I must be alone now. But fetch word on the questioning of the queen. Are these rumors of her past true? When you know, seek me out for a private audience and do not tell anyone what you learn."

"Yes, Majesty. At once."

Again, all alone to think about things. There were so many unreliable sources at court. My mother—I was always closer to her than my father—often reminded me how much I resembled Edward IV, my grandfather. Either with my resemblance or my wit and charms, she'd told me. "Rule, Henry, rule, and if there are obstacles to your throne and line of heirs, remove them. But also rule your people with kindness and gentleness to earn their loyalty. Rule in fear, and one day it will bite you, destroying everything. It is what I told your father, and I tell it to you, for one day you will be king, taking his place. In your veins runs the blood of both Tudor and York, and you are more York than you think. Know the truth of who you are." I may have been my father's heir when he ruled after Arthur's death, but I was my mother's son. I would rule, and I would think independently of what people told me to do. But I knew there were some things in common between my father and I. Perhaps through me, it would be a united England. But what of my heirs? It couldn't end with me. I knew I was not as young as I used to be.

As I thought about this, Charles came in. His head hung in sadness and worry.

"Your Grace. Thomas Culpepper said you would be angry that I came instead of him despite your command. But he felt I might do better than him in speaking with you because he felt himself too young for such matters."

I knew something was wrong when Culpepper was not with him. But since I was in a reminiscent mood, I nodded to Charles and ushered him to tell me what was happening.

"Your Grace, I bid you directness. The queen's past is ultimately true and has now come to light as a way of haunting her. Though I urge you first, the questioning of her character since marrying you must go further, as there are other rumors that her behavior continues and others are involved. I know you are fond of the young girl, and I'm sure she could bear you an heir. She was brought to you to bring you out of your sulky temperament by the last queen. I beg you humbly to have her questioned further and others. But I think, if I may be bold, a trip to visit a friend you can trust is in order. I hear you can enjoy some games at Hever Castle if you are well enough to travel tomorrow."

Hearing from Charles, what he suggested, softened my mood some. Not just some, but enough. I didn't have to be there as they questioned her, but I hoped they were wrong about the rumors of her character today. I cared for her, even if I couldn't stand her childlike ways all the time.

I nodded. "Make the preparations, Charles, and I ask that you go with me. I could use the company. We will travel light. But send word to Hever Castle to make ready for guests. We will stay for about a week, and then you will travel back here to be with family and oversee the situation with Catherine. Send word to Cranmer that he must find who these 'others' are and investigate quickly."

Charles replied, "Yes, Majesty. All will be done. Shall I ask Thomas Culpepper to join us in attendance at Hever Castle? You will need servants."

"No. Have a different servant attend me for the travel and pick a small guard unit. I have no worry for fear when visiting Anne. Oh, to see Anne. Perhaps she will tell me her thoughts of Catherine, no?"

Chapter Five

Killer King — November 1541
Anne

I listened as the messenger sent from Henry's court said urgently that important guests were coming to visit and play at one of my popular game parties. He kept the message brief as we were not alone, so I dismissed my ladies and asked one of them, Jane, to bring refreshments and to prepare a room for the messenger to rest before carrying back my message. The messenger was thankful, and when we were alone, he took a ring from his pocket. A ring that only I would recognize, as it was something I had given to Henry when we were married. I took the ring and offered the chair, so I could hear his message. I knew Henry liked games, and I understood his meaning.

The messenger took the drink offered to him and spoke after we were alone again. Henry did not want a letter sent this time. That was obvious as the messenger spoke slowly, remembering each word.

"My Mistress Anne, beloved sister. Sir Charles and I will arrive quickly in disguise and wish to spend time with you. Tell your household, but urge the secrecy of this visit. I will not have rumors spread about my visit to harm your reputation or that of your ladies, but I need a long night of a game of cards. I do not wish to impose but will be humbled when you open the door to us."

I know I had not been here long, almost two years, but my English had improved steadily. I respectfully asked the messenger to tell me quietly about the news of the court and His Majesty. I didn't wish to make him uncomfortable, but I could sense there was trouble at court. I only hoped that Catherine had not died unexpectedly or anything.

"Lady Anne, if I tell you of the court's news, please do not let His Majesty know I said more than what I should have."

I promised.

"It seems rumors about Queen Catherine's very colorful past have made it to the king's ears. From what I know, he has had her arrested and questioned. It turns out she was very solicitous with her body prior to coming to court to serve in your household when you were queen. But, alas, the king has been given other news. She may have already been married before coming to court. So, the king is disheartened and rightly upset. Sir Charles recommended a visit to Hever Castle to see you and to enjoy a card game. Amongst the servants, we know she brought life back to him, but we are unsure if she will be forgiven, for she is so young and immature, and we are afraid, as some would say, she is destined for the block. But he has been in pain a lot and has grown weary of the queen, too. If I can say something more, my lady, there are people in the court that miss your sweet and gentle nature. We often hoped that the king would reconsider the annulment because you were always so kind and gracious. We need that at court when the king is not feeling boisterous because of his leg."

I smiled, realizing this was one of the nicest things I had heard other than from my ladies telling me the same. I could feel my cheeks becoming rosy. Rather than have the messenger be self-conscious about my embarrassment, I told him that one of my ladies would show him where to freshen up before returning to Henry's court. However, my embarrassment didn't go away as quickly as I thought. In fact, I was feeling faint. That was not like me. I would've collapsed had it not been for the messenger catching me and calling for my ladies.

I took ill upon hearing the news that Catherine was being interrogated for her past, and having seen what I had in the court and knowing Henry, I was not feeling well. But Henry and Charles were on their way for a visit. I was sent to bed to rest. Lady Jane took care of the messenger and sent him back to court, sending word that we would be ready when the guests arrived. After all, I had just told her we were to expect company. Because I could trust her service, she did not pose questions as to their identities. But I felt my ladies knew about the endearing friendship I'd maintained with the king, especially when England knew me as his beloved sister.

After some hours of rest, I felt better and worked with my ladies on preparing the estate for the games and their arrival. My household, I learned quickly, loved to entertain, and I loved my gambling vice.

As the day progressed, I heard someone in the reception room whispering to Lady Jane and Lady Elizabeth. I could only make out certain mumblings, but as I listened carefully, some villagers were asking for spare bread, as taxes took most of their income. I immediately made myself presentable and joined the conversation. Listening to the villagers speak and seeing some of the hungry children, I knelt down to one of the little ones. Moving a hair that blocked her blue eyes from being seen, I saw she had the sweetest dimples, almost reminding me of Princess Elizabeth. Noticing dirt smudges on her cheek, I took a handkerchief from my dress and wiped it clean, raising a giggle from her.

"My, we are a tad dirty, aren't we?"

The little girl looked up at me and smiled. "Yes, my lady. I'm sorry I am not clean."

"Hush, child. My ladies will give you a nice, warm bath. Would you like that? And I'm sure we can find something sweet to eat while I talk to your parents. Go on now. Go with them." Turning to my ladies, I said, "Find a couple of dresses that were in Elizabeth's room while I have refreshments with their parents."

I showed the family to the parlor and poured the refreshments myself. The mother was in tears at the kindness I had shown them so far, and she held onto her husband's arm. I listened to their burdens and thought about how best to help them. I could help them—I had the means right now—but what if they needed more? Perhaps I could speak to Henry? First things first, I had Henry coming with Charles for a rest and whatever else His Majesty requested, but I had this family here.

I called for one of my ladies to fetch my coin purse. While she did that, I spoke to the husband and wife. "I will help you, but I will do more than that. I will speak with the king and ask what is happening. If you are suffering, others might be as well. I don't go out much, but how is the health in the town?"

"Lady Anne, it is sufficient but not perfect. The baker's wife came down with the sweating sickness, or so we thought, but then it passed. Their child just had an unusual rash and fever but is feeling better now. These new taxes the king is imposing are going to hurt all of us, but we are afraid of the tax collector and the penalties that lie behind it. We respect the king, but the beheadings are too much."

I pondered on their words as my right hand reached for my neck, making me realize I could've been one more beheading that Henry had become known for. I'd lost count of how many people had lost their heads already. Henry had just executed his own mother's first cousin, Margaret Pole, earlier that year. The elderly countess was sixty-seven years old, and as I understood it, she even helped to look after Henry when he was a young child. Deep down, I had a feeling I would have to be careful talking to Henry about these concerns, but my thoughts were interrupted by my guests.

"If I beg your pardon, my lady, it is with a deep and saddened heart that I tell you that King Henry is becoming known to some parts as 'The Killer King,' It is such a shame because the people love His Majesty, but we are afraid of— how should we say—his moods the last several years. We want our king to be content with us, but if we share our concerns, we may all lose our heads."

The man's words stung me because I knew it to be the truth. Before I knew it, the children came running back to show off their dresses. Each had a doll that they found amongst Elizabeth's things, but I had no heart to take the dolls away from them. The family thanked me for my kindness and headed home after my promise to help them. I also informed them I was expecting guests and must make preparations, but not before I knelt before the girls and told them to visit the kitchen before leaving, as I was sure there were some sweets waiting for them. I received hugs in return, and it made me think about how much I wished the marriage would have welcomed a child for Henry and me. But God had other intentions for us both. As usual, I was lost in thought and time went by until one of my ladies brought me news that the hour was getting late, and that a light supper was set for us in the garden.

We feasted on pigeon and other things, but my mind was still clouded with news of what the couple had called Henry. I could speak to him—or would he be in one of his moods? Another messenger brought me a letter from my mother, the seventh in the last few months. She continued to write about how I should return home, as she was missing me and wanted me to tend to her, as she felt my brother was not handling the family affairs the way she expected since our father's death. It was the same thoughts over and over. I had written to her a few months ago saying I was happy in England, and that even though my marriage to the king was over, I was honored due my station as his beloved sister.

I took the letter and destroyed it later, like all the others. Enough misery thinking! Henry was coming, and that was all that mattered to me.

Ever since I agreed to Henry's terms and helped plan our agreement with things, my friendship with had Henry blossomed. Though we seemed to talk about many things more now than when we were married, one thing remained true. He was a king to be trusted, despite the upsetting rumors of people and what some would consider being his flaws. We all have flaws, but it is up to us and our conscience to rise above them. I knew, from my time in court, to not pose a difference in matters he paid the most attention to, especially with religious beliefs, questions about his decisions, or the lack of male heirs to follow him. The man I knew to be Henry was jovial, but a man that could anger. But he had a powerful belief in who he was.

As the evening progressed, I retired early, but with only two of my ladies in confidence. It was with them I could trust my most secret thoughts about my person, my being, everything, and knew they would not betray me. I felt the others might sense a tad of jealousy as this could look like favoritism, but I rewarded them with other signs of loyalty and affection to avoid any questioning. I took with me to my rooms Lady Eleanor and Lady Jane. With them, I could just speak and sometimes that helped, as I was still learning the English language.

"Ladies, I wondered if you've heard the rumors of what the good people of England are now calling the king? The family that was here earlier referred to him as the 'Killer King.' I find it disturbing, but I know that is part of his sense of justice. Tell me."

Lady Jane shifted from one side to the other and looked rather uneasy, but she nodded as her eyes pointed downward to the floor. There was no getting around this nickname the king had earned somehow. Lady Jane added, "There are rumors in the court that his queen has been untrue since the marriage, and before he wedded her, she was... um...a whore, but not the king's whore or the king's great whore. In fact, my lady, she was a whore before she became part of your household. We were not sure if you were aware, as you were new to England."

My hand fluttered toward my throat as I felt a lump and could not breathe. My head felt like it was spinning, and my heart was pounding. Perhaps I was to blame for having her as one of my ladies, but I did not know of her improper past. But I begged Jane to continue with all the news that would help me understand the reasons for the king's visit.

"It is said that the queen has been most untrue to the king, and that she shows no signs of child even given the number of times he has visited her. But the king is also in a foul mood, as his legs are giving him immense pain that only Thomas Culpepper can remedy. The king's physicians are irrelevant with Thomas Culpepper. As his station, he has complete access to the king's ear, and they say in the court that Thomas Culpepper is one man who has been influenced by the queen and visits her. The king shows no sign of knowing this, but with court gossip, he might just know. Oh, my lady, are you all right with the court news I have shared? I worry about your sensitive nature, and how the king might treat you if you fall out of favor."

I laughed at her innocence. "Lady Jane, do not fret, for Henry and I understand each other on all matters, and a promise he has yet to keep when I ask this of him. Do not worry, as before I wedded Henry, I learned some insights into not upsetting him I know how to use. Plus, Henry is a kind soul, sometimes misunderstood. I know secrets that Henry shares with me in confidence, and I can say that while I will not betray his inner feelings, he is misunderstood a lot by those he trusts most. But we must trust in Henry's journey and his calling by God to always do the right thing. Is there more news of the court that we must know before his arrival? All must be ready if Henry is to remain calm and seek peace for right now."

Both my ladies shook their head that there was no other news. All the court could think about was Queen Catherine's infidelities before and during the marriage. They also spoke of no pregnancy that should have happened by now. I could feel it in my heart that Henry's option would be to give Queen Catherine the same fate as Anne Boleyn. If this happened, would this be my chance for a reconciliation? Could this be the promise I could ask of Henry, though it was not the one I wanted at first? I slept on it, for Henry would be there in the next few days, and there was still a lot of work to do.

Chapter Six

Promises and Desires — December 1541
Henry and Anne

I awoke that day with the same excitement I had all those months before, when it was what Henry and I jokingly called the day we were both born anew. To the eyes of the court, it was our annulment day. It seemed so long ago, but in reality it wasn't. So much had happened since that day. We'd become closer than before, Henry confided in me things he couldn't tell others, especially Charles, and the way he had no quarrel if the young Elizabeth wanted to spend time with me. I couldn't be happier with the way things turned out, but secretly, I waited for the one perfect moment in which I could beg His Majesty for the promise he'd made to me. My head spun with thoughts of what I could ask for and not seem like a vicious woman out to gain more than what I already had been given. But my heart had other thoughts, and I realized it was because of my heart and common sense that the annulment had benefited me. My mother, in her fears, had thought shielding us daughters from a proper education to rule alongside our husbands was best, but as I saw Elizabeth progress in her studies, the way Henry was truly proud of her, I realized my mother was wrong. How could I do better for the rest of my life?

As I was getting dressed, there was a forceful knock on my door. It was a pageboy, the cook's youngest son, and such a lovely child. "Miss Anne, Miss Anne! Can I come in?"

"Yes, Little John. You may come in. I am dressed, just fixing my hair to greet the day."

Little John was how we referred to him, not to confuse him with his father, who also served in my household. John was a pleasant five-year-old, and though quite young to be a pageboy, I wanted him to spend as much time as he could with his parents. His mother was one of the best cooks I had ever met, and when we dined in the evenings, we all ate together. Little John had many exciting stories to tell. He was one reason my heart knew what to ask of Henry when the time was right.

Short of breath, he excitedly told me that Henry and some other man had arrived, and in between words, he took several deep breaths. As I listened, I could put two and two together. Once he finished telling me about what Henry wore and how excited he was to be here, I offered him some licorice and thanked him for being the best pageboy I'd ever had. I told him I wanted him to play for the rest of the day and to have fun because there would be plenty of work in the days ahead for our guests. But today, he just needed to be a little boy. He smiled and was happy to hear it, so happy that I got a well-earned hug from him. My ladies gasped, as I did not realize his hands were a little dirty and a smudge hit my cheek.

"Come now, we were all little children once. Bring me a handkerchief and I will have this off quickly. But Little John, thank you for your affection. If you find me later, I will give you more licorice. With your parents' permission, of course."

"Yes, ma'am. I will ask my mama. She always says yes to me."

We laughed as he barreled out of the room, and I finished getting ready.

"My, Henry is a bit early. Lady Jane, see to his needs and show him and Charles where they will sleep while here. But I know this castle will remind his majesty of Anne Boleyn and her family, so be careful in your words. Tell the men that I will join them shortly and we can enjoy refreshments."

Lady Katharine continued to assist me in becoming presentable. As she looked at my gown, she frowned. Ever since I met her and took her into my service, she had been the first person who hoped my marriage to Henry would last, as she saw how easily I could manage his moods. "My Grace, that color will not do today. Let's change into your green dress, as the necklace the king gave you back in July would match perfectly. And if I remember correctly, His Majesty favors the color."

I quickly changed into the green one, and the necklace was placed around my neck. I also put on the rings and broch that Henry had gifted to me. I just hoped it wasn't too much, and on second thought, I removed the broch and only wore one ring. Simple. I also suggested that Lady Katharine head downstairs and prepare the game room for us. A party was planned for later in the week for the town, but if needed, I could adjust the event. Or perhaps Henry would enjoy some lively moments in one of his towns. But first I must greet my guests. My stomach was a little upset, but probably because I longed to see Henry and Charles.

I rushed down the stairs to find myself bowed to by two such great friends. I simply curtsied, paying respect, but Charles extended his arms as if to hug me. Normally this would not have happened in public, but it was just the three of us. And definitely not proper protocol, as Charles was beneath Henry, but he did not mind one bit. Henry, being next, turned to give me a hug.

"Sister, I have missed you."

Somehow, I giggled each time I heard myself referred to as "sister." But I acknowledged that I'd missed him as well. Time had made us grow fonder of all things. I embraced both Henry and Charles and asked about their health and well-being, but that was when Henry chided me for worrying about him, when it was he who should worry about me being all alone in the castle. I thought Hever Castle brought out some unfortunate and mistaken feelings about what had happened with Anne Boleyn.

My ladies joined us for refreshments and Henry asked after them. They all replied that all was well, and in fact, there was less formality in this household than in the king's household to ease his mind should there be any distasteful gossip, as one never knew what circulated in the court. Henry relaxed and became less formal, including laughing and making crude jokes, forgetting he was in the company of ladies. This was how Henry truly was. Magnificent and powerful as any king, but a man. When Henry could be himself without criticism, you could see his gentleness — something he must have inherited from his mother, the late Queen Elizabeth.

"Henry, Charles, I have set up some games and drinks in the card room if you wish to play, or we could just visit for a bit, but I understand if you have other things to attend to while you are here. I am at Your Majesty's service."

Charles laughed and said jokingly, "Henry, you must have not told Lady Anne the reason we are here. She thinks it to be all about business."

We laughed merrily at the remark, and somehow, my ladies took it upon themselves to leave us alone. I knew why they were there, and so did my ladies. It was to let Henry be Henry, as he had asked in his letter to me. The cook entered the room with a plate loaded with fruit, breads, and cheese. She said, "For tonight, I have prepared a small feast, and if you wish for privacy to dine, Mistress Anne, let me know and I shall prepare the kitchen rooms for the household. And thank you for spoiling Little John with several pieces of licorice, but you shouldn't have. Do you have a need for him today? He mentioned something, but you know how he is when he's excited. I didn't quite catch his meaning. Your Graces." She bowed to the men.

"That won't be necessary. We will all dine together tonight as usual, if that is all right with His Majesty and Sir Charles. And Little John gets to be a child today. I was going to have him tend to His Majesty starting tomorrow, if that is okay with you. He might enjoy a change of pace instead of always being with the ladies."

Henry smiled at the words and how affectionate my household was toward me. He spoke to all in the room. "I would be much obliged if Lady Anne's household did not change their usual customs because I am here. As you can see, I am without guard and my royal entourage, and just want to visit, laugh, and get to know you all. In fact, please send for this 'Little John' to come to me. I shall like to make his acquaintance, as he sounds very important."

The cook, Sadie, nodded and left to bring her son to us. This was the Henry I came to know more and more after the marriage ended. I noticed he limped heavily, more than before, but I knew his pride would not allow me to make a fuss over him. Instead, I simply brought a stool toward him where he could rest his leg more easily. No words needed to be said about making his comfort my priority. He nodded and reached to hold my hand. He clasped it with a firm tenderness in all signs of affection that he could allow himself to show. Sir Charles coughed lightly and offered to excuse himself, leaving us alone.

Henry was dazed a little before speaking. I listened as I watched his body language. I wanted to be sure I understood what he must be thinking.

"Anne, it is so good that you have welcomed us into your home. I hope you are finding life in Hever Castle fitting for you. But this place haunts me. I feel I could tell you what ails me, and you won't be my judgment in any of this. May I?"

"Alas, Henry, I only wish to see your happiness. Do you remember when we discussed our separation plans, and I told you I am your most humble servant? That still holds true to this day. Tell me what causes you such distress. I know you must have gone to great lengths to hide your travels to me from your own council. Otherwise, why all the secrecy? Know I only ask to understand what troubles you and how I can help you."

Henry shifted in his seat, showing signs of being uncomfortable at the slight confrontation, but he knew me well enough to know I meant no harm to his person. He stared out the window, lost in thought, as he didn't say a word. Instead, I could see a single tear flow down his cheek. Witnessing this, my heart melted. The weight of the world, England and more, must weigh on his soul, clutching every breath he took.

"Oh, God has burdened my soul. My sons don't live to inherit my throne. I have one, but for how long? I am cursed, I tell you, and not one of my council seeks to agree with me. Sometimes I think I see my mother, and she is whispering to me to break some curse. I share my thoughts with Charles, but he doesn't understand what I understand. What it means to be king. But I don't want to trouble you, sweet sister. How about a game?"

I knew he would tell me in his own time, but usually games helped the mood. He was definitely melancholy, and I wondered if it had to do with the gossip of Queen Catherine and her life as a harlot. With Henry one had to exhibit patience so he opened up his feelings, and then he could understand what he needed most. I smiled so he would see my endearment toward his sensitive side. I rose from my chair and placed my hands on his shoulders.

"Dearest Henry. The world is at your fingertips, but it is God who will reward those who are strong in their faith and serve him. Your council serves you, but your personal heart suffers because you trust no one closest to you to share this burden. I understand why, after all this time. Let me tell you a secret about my upbringing. In Germany, my mother did not believe us girls to be worthy of our husbands, but my father did. We may not have been formally educated the way your daughter Elizabeth is today, or how Mary was taught so many wondrous things, but my father made sure we learned the ways of the world by watching him with his council. I share this secret with you because I truly feel you can trust in me with your secrets. I hear things among your people now that I live away from the court and am no longer queen. I cherish these thoughts so that one day, when you need it most, I can provide you comfort. This will be hard to hear, sweet Henry.

"I hear the rumors of the court, what the people call you behind your back. You are no fool. I know you hear it too, somehow. We'll get to the root of what truly bothers you and makes you a restless spirit. But as you said, let's play. I will listen when you need it most and offer what comfort I can."

Henry remained silent while we played, which was always the case. He at least knew I was there for him as a person and not as his royal self. He then interrupted the silence with a soft, "How I wish you would have known my mother. You and she are much alike. She had a way with my father when he was in one of his moods, too. But that is not for this moment. Tell me, Anne, what is your secret desire that you wanted to ask of me? I pray tell that I have one of my own, yet I am humbled to have it remain a secret."

It took me moments to gather up the courage, but I was

ready to ask for my desire. "Henry, I know I am not the wife you wanted, but I wish to be a mother. I don't want a husband to control me or bear me ill will because of my station." I paused to gather up more courage to ask this of a gentle man and my king. "Will you give me a child? You do not need to call this child yours or ruin your son's claim to the throne. I will live my life peacefully with my child, only to be blessed knowing that you are man enough to father as many children as the stars in the sky. I am your loyal and humble servant."

Henry was quiet for about a minute or two, before a tear fell from his eye. He reached for my hand and grasped it tightly in his.

"Sweet Anne, I will come to you while I am here. I will bed you, my sweet Anne. The truth of this is I was going to ask you to lie with me, to make me feel whole again. I realized that I miss you at court, and we are better now than we were before. I feared in asking you, as I did not want to tarnish my lady's reputation. Maybe time is what has brought us closer, don't you think?"

I smiled at Henry, brought his hand to my lips, and kissed it. It took me by surprise that we might have learned to love each other after all this time. Henry was a man that would take anyone by surprise, including me.

And with that, we played all day until Charles rejoined us late in the afternoon.

Chapter Seven

Feelings — December 1541
Henry and Anne

It had been almost a full week since Henry arrived, and the house had never seemed livelier since I took residence. I'd hosted two large games with townspeople that I could trust, who would allow both the king and Sir Charles privacy but entertainment. Though I turned the other way, I knew Charles had entertained a few ladies, while Henry and I had shared quiet moments together, just talking and laughing.

And then it happened. Henry came to my rooms and dismissed my ladies, and announced that he would spend the evening with me, much to my surprise.

"Anne, I swear, I am at a crossroads in my life. How much do you remember about my family history? Or have I not shared that part of me with you?"

"Sweet Henry, I know enough to understand that your

mother loved you above all things, your lady grandmother, the king's mother, was pious and strict but adored you, and that no matter how hard you tried to be your own man, your father, King Henry VII, was vigilant in how you should act since you were the only heir after Arthur. I know things were hard, and many people may not understand you and your true nature. Did I miss anything?"

Henry laughed. It was so good to hear him laugh and be happy. "I fear that no matter what wife I choose, I am going to end up parting with them somehow. Either with their loss of life, divorce, or something. But you, you are so different. You accepted the fate. I know we talked about it last year, but I feel you are the only one I can believe who truly understands me. I loved Katherine, my late brother's widow. I thought she and I would build a nation that God would truly feel blessed by, but part of me is torn among the religious faiths. My heart seems torn, but I don't know. I don't know about this second Catherine, for she is young. How did I not see her harlot ways? God must punish me, I swear. I command the good of England in his name. I have been his faithful servant, and yet, I can bear no sons that will live."

I moved closer to Henry, intending to be supportive, but as I was standing right next to him, his arm gripped my waist so tightly that I gave a little startle. His hand moved from my side toward my thigh, and with a little nudge, he made me fall into his lap. While this was the most affection I had seen from him since our marriage, my heart fluttered. I let him take the lead because one, he was Henry, and two, I was happy with this. As I sat on his lap, I could sense his vulnerability because he was soft-hearted when he whispered my name. He was sincere and not so demanding. It was as if he was experiencing a moment of tenderness with me. As much as I still loved Henry, I followed his lead to what he needed. He did not need another woman upsetting him. I was giddy inside, as I loved Henry still, and when his mouth met mine, I just melted into the kiss. We kissed like we never had before, full of passion and tenderness. We embraced for the longest time until Henry led me to his rooms.

Breaking the silence, he whispered, "It would be best here, as I'm sure your beautiful rooms should remain with your honor. I vow to you my discretion in the matter ahead of us at this moment. I will not have you tarnished."

And with that, we shared our night together in the house's silence. I knew my ladies would wonder where I was, but they were women after all, so they would understand this secret of ours. By the time morning came, I found myself still in love with Henry, but knew I must keep my secret hidden in my heart at all costs. Henry must be Henry.

I watched him sleep awhile before I left a note to join me for breakfast or anything. I knew better than to cling to him like everyone else did. Sometimes I wondered why people wouldn't let Henry just be Henry, so to speak. I guess that was the price for being king, and it certainly made me feel even better about our marriage ending. I had been educated in the ways of trysts in the bedroom more than when I was first married. Lady Jane saw to that tutelage, as my first thinking was it would just happen because he kissed me good night and good morning each time we lay together. How naïve I must have been. But now I was more worldly, or at least I thought so. I found my hand wandering to my belly and wondered, but not after just one time. I couldn't be. This would definitely not be in the cards for Henry or me, but I wondered.

I returned to my rooms and immediately called for a rose bath. I had read that this was a relaxing way to cleanse the body from a night of wondrous bliss. My ladies immediately drew the bath and left me alone, except for Lady Jane. She was full of questions, but I did my best to answer them truthfully. I told her that the king's happiness was more important than my own, and if he felt any desire last night, it was his right. She smiled, but cautioned me to be careful.

"Lady Anne, I must ask you to take great care. I have grown rather fond of you, and think of you dearly. Let no harm come to you, mistress."

Because she was a lady of protocol, this was as much affection as she could entertain. I loved her more for it. As I lay in the bath's warmth, thoughts ran through my head about the repercussions of last night, but were soon dismissed when Lady Jane entered the bathing chamber from the other room.

"Lady, I was tending to the dusting of the rooms when a piece of the wall cracked. I know this sounds ridiculous, but I then removed all the pieces to see I cut myself even," she said. "There was this jewel box hidden in the wall. Could it be from when the Boleyn family lived here? This is so exciting, and I didn't open the box but came directly here."

I stood from my bath, seeing how it ended early because of such excitement. I loved games and thought perhaps this was a game to be played. I urged my ladies to dress me quickly, but to do their best, as I was excited to examine the jewel box. I could be quite vain being a woman and all, but still young at heart, and I loved a pleasurable excitement now and again.

Seeing how I was presentable finally, I let Lady Jane show me the jewel box. My mind ran in a hundred different directions, questioning what on earth it could all mean.

The jewelry box was a solid green with gold trim, and it looked like it would require a key, but it was unlocked. Carefully, holding our breaths, we opened it. My ladies seemed to enjoy these mysteries as well. We looked inside, and in it was a parchment, like a letter. On the outside of the folded letter was a beautifully written "E.". I wondered if "E" meant Elizabeth.

Everyone waited for me. I took the letter out of the box and handed it to Lady Katharine. My spoken language wasn't that good yet to read something as amazing as this might be.

"Please read this for us. I am worried my English isn't quite up to snuff yet." I giggled at my skill in the language.

Lady Katharine took the letter, and we all gathered around to hear her.

My darling Elizabeth,

If you are reading this letter, then you must be old enough to have lived a life without me in it as your mother. I write this letter to you as I await my maker, but have given this letter plus some special secrets to a friend I could trust to make a game for you. But before you play, do not hate your father, the king, for his sentence upon my life. Somehow, I'd failed him in bearing him a son, and as you must know by now, sons are so important. But that doesn't make you less of a person because you are a woman. You are your father's daughter. You have his hair coloring, his eyes, and I knew from the minute you were born, your attitude is a combination of your father's powerful will and my tenacity. Love your father the best you can. If there are no heirs to keep his line, earn his favor somehow to become queen in your right one day. This I have seen through other sources. I will not reveal them to you, but know it is in your power to one day rule England. Stay true to your heart and make England love you. Serve the land, serve the people. I leave to you, my daughter, the jewels I was given by your father. I never returned these when I fell out of His Grace's favor. Instead, I asked one of my ladies to keep them safe for you. Visit Lady Anne Zouche. Find her and tell her the title, "The Obedience of a Christian Man" and she will return to you what is truly rightfully yours. Then find Lady Margaret Dymoke and tell her the phrase, "The master of the horse will ride at midnight" and she will give unto you my letters and wisdom that will enable you to be stronger than any other woman in the country. In addition, you will receive my emerald ring, a sign of the Boleyn legacy. You are Boleyn and you are Tudor. May God forgive my soul for speaking heresy to you, but I have been told that you will be queen of England, but you need these items from my ladies, who served me well, in order to fulfill your destiny. Let no man control your mind, body, and soul, and remember these words: You are your father's daughter. There is a reason he separated from the papacy. Honor the Church of England and your father.

 Just like your father, you were born from two worlds to become one. Unite and save England from the clutches of those so devout that they lose their own conscience.

 With this, I bid you my love eternal as your mother, and am ready to return to the arms of God.

 Your loving mother,
Anne Boleyn

We all had tears in our eyes as we finished reading the

letter from a loving mother to her daughter. I knew better than to share this letter with Henry, for I knew not what he would think, but felt it was my duty to help ensure that Elizabeth should retrieve these beautiful possessions that were left for her. However, I wondered if Elizabeth would ever be queen of England one day, as her mother stated. If that were to be true, then Elizabeth would need a strong education and upbringing, but balanced out to avoid suspicion. But what of Mary? Mary was already a young woman, beautiful, and with a strong faith, sometimes a faith so strong it blinded her in matters of the heart. But that was my humble opinion, and only an opinion. I must see that she one day found happiness in a loving marriage.

From the hall I could hear a man's voice, loud as could be, and I sent one of my ladies to inquire while the rest of us looked through the letter once more. I examined the jewelry box and found a secret compartment underneath the velvet material that lined the inside. I had Lady Jane find me a pair of scissors, and carefully I made some slight cuts to open it further. In the lining was another note, simple and sweet. But there was more. Feeling around the box, I came across a ring—a woman's ring—that looked to be elegant and rather beautiful. I decided that this was something I must see that Elizabeth got when a little older. I then wondered how much she truly knew about her mother and father. Knowing I wasn't the current queen or her parent, I felt it my duty to help guide her in life.

"Lady Jane, place these treasures in one of my chests, so no one knows of this. It is truly paramount that we keep silent about what we found this morning. Freshen up, ladies, and let's see to the king and Sir Charles."

I hurried out to greet the king, who obviously was awake now and causing a minor commotion with some members of the household. Ironically, I found it charming because the ruckus only involved a young child and the king playing as if they were knights on a battlefield. Pillows were strewn all over the parlor room and things were in disarray, but to see Henry so happy made me feel pleased I could offer him some comfort. I watched the two play until they were joined by Sir Charles.

Keeping my distance, I still watched the two grown men playing with the child as if they did not know their maturity. It was as heartfelt as could be, considering I knew Henry's pains, both physically and emotionally. Deep in my heart, I wished secretly that he would want to give us another chance at marriage and a happy life. I might even be a mother then! Knowing this month was also December, this would also mark the first year of the new law: the Unlawful Games Act. Henry, earlier in the year, decreed that no games but archery would be played on Christmas Day, so that would mean a day without the card games we planned to host. Well, at least we could celebrate together should Henry choose to stay or return to his castle, and I thought he would choose the latter knowing him. He loved this holiday to be celebrated lavishly, but I wondered how this Christmas would feel to him.

As I approached the playful trio, I politely inquired to Henry if he would like to stay for the holiday or if he felt the court needed him more. The smile in his eyes said what his heart wanted, but the words did not match the meaning. I knew his court needed him, but as my kind heart would tell him, I just sought his happiness. But he promised to return, and before he left, he spent many nights with me.

Chapter Eight

Secrets — May 1542
Anne

Though it's been months since Henry left from his secret visit, a reminder of him remained behind. I rose from the chair and peeked out the window to watch the young children play in the gardens. I allowed the children to play in the castle grounds whenever their hearts desired. My right hand caressed my swollen belly, the reminder that Henry had left behind. I never had time to tell him about all that was happening with the queen. I knew it was only a matter of time before fate befell her in some form or another.

I heard from Charles, though. He sent letters about the affairs of the court, his family life, and how Henry fared, though I didn't pry. But I enjoyed hearing anything about Henry. I learned he'd been in a foul mood as of late, so Charles thought I might send a note to brighten his spirits.

Thinking about this, I had a much better idea. An idea that caused me to giggle. But it would require a certain young boy from the kitchen to help me, and some training in the game! I found Little John running around playing with the chickens, so I asked him to spend a little time with me each morning over the next two days so I could teach him one of the king's favorite games.

Because Henry and I loved food and household things, which no one really paid attention to, we sometimes offered different cooks to each other's kitchens so we could experience treats here and there. I thought it was time to have a borrowing session so Little John could play with the king. I wrote back my idea to Charles and began making preparations with the cook and Little John. A swapping of the cooks would be perfect to let Henry know he was loved, no matter how much in despair he might feel with Catherine having met with the executioner. I went to speak to Little John about the upcoming visit.

"Little John, mind if I steal you away from the other children again for just a moment?"

He came running and, while panting, asked if it was time for another game. I laughed and told him he had mastered the game to play with the king, and all he needed to do was just be himself and make the king giggle like he did when they were here.

The day was soon upon us that my lovely cook and her son would travel to Henry's castle. I stopped by to see her as she was kneading the bread. She looked at me and my growing belly.

"Madame, off your feet! You should not be here in the

kitchen at all. Rest! But let me get you something to drink first. I am just preparing a few things I know you will enjoy while I am away, and I have asked a dear friend of mine from the town to cook in my place. I know you have others, but in your condition, we must take care."

She must have seen my eyes grow wide in fear that people would wonder about this secret growing inside me. She ran over and placed her hands over mine. The flour turned my hands white.

"No, child, do not fret. I can trust my friend to not share your condition with anyone, for I helped her with similar situations. I know you know I am much older than I should be to have a young child such as Little John. His mother could not provide for him the way I can, as you can see. His mother is my friend who will fill in for me while I am at court. She understands. In fact, Little John's real father is another lord that cannot claim him. This is the fate of us women, it seems. So, rest easy and do not fret. Just think, you went from mistress to madame in a short period, and have had your heart's fondest wish come true. It's how we say, matters of the heart. You will enjoy her cooking, but I am leaving you a few things I know you and your ladies will enjoy while we are away."

A tear of happiness rolled down my cheek, and I wiped it away with one of my flour hands, smudging flour onto my cheek. My household was so special to me that I just hoped they would love this child of mine as much as I did. My ladies had been preparing a special nursery for this baby and keeping me occupied, so I didn't ruin their surprise.

In my pocket I felt the little purse I had forgotten to give her the other day. "I have this for you and Little John while you are there. I want him to enjoy things like other children at the court and not have his heart broken. Please see he gets little treats here and there. But I ask of you, please do not tell the king of my condition. I will…I will tell him in good time. I don't want him to think I am relishing in the death of the last queen, for I am not."

The cook brought me a glass of warm milk, which was supposed to soothe the baby, and a plate of breads and some sweets. I preferred the sweets right now more than the breads, but I ate from both. I used this time with us two alone to share something I had been thinking about with her.

"What if I am not an excellent mother? I don't know the first thing about being a mother and what to do. It's not like I'm a queen or have royal nannies to assist me. I must raise this child, the king's child, alone and in secret. But I am not bitter. I am overjoyed to have a brief part of Henry inside me, and when this child is born, I will love him ever so much."

The cook nodded and touched my shoulder as if she were my mother. "Child, you will be an exceptional mother to this special child. I know you didn't ask me, but I want you to have something. I will have it delivered to your room later today. I need to finish baking. But, take my gift and use it for the child. A warm blanket is always needed for the little ones. I worked on it each night since I saw you were with the child. But I will keep your secret from the king. If he asks how you are, I will simply say to him you are joyous with the new year of life, health, and happiness. All of which is true."

I continued to eat the sweets and the breads while watching this lovely woman bake. Before I knew it, a knock was heard at the kitchen door. She wiped her hands on her skirt and went to open the door, greeting her friend.

"I'm so glad you stopped by. Our kitchen is just ready for your delicious goodies while I am away. Come in, dear. I want you to meet Mistress Anne. Come, let me take your shawl and get you a cool drink."

I put my treat down and tried to stand up, but as I did so, the little one inside me kicked because he or she must have loved the treat so much. Out of habit like I normally did, I cradled my hand around my belly as if to calm the baby, and then I greeted the young woman.

"Sit, ma'am. Call me Gretchen. I hope you don't mind my cooking for you and your household while she's away for a bit. I promise you I am a wonderful cook, and I can make anything you would like. If I can, may I ask how far along you are, so I know if there are spices or herbs I should avoid? I am also a midwife should you have any discomfort."

I smiled at her friendliness. I didn't even know how far along I was. I had to learn about relations and the effects through the experiences of others, for when I was married, Henry did not touch me until after our marriage was ended, and only during his last visit.

"Sit, both of you ladies. Let's visit a bit, shall we?"

I welcomed Gretchen with open arms into my household. Being sure we three were alone, I locked the doors to the kitchen, but not before sending word to Lady Mary that we wished not to be disturbed under any circumstances, but that all was well. I was just in need of some advice about my current condition and wanted my ladies to focus on the surprise they were creating for me.

"Gretchen, I have been told I can trust you. I don't know how far along I am. I guess you could say that I am naïve in that area, all things considered, being a virgin during my marriage to the king and such. I know it has been several months, but I am not sure. Do you think you could do me this service and find out? Then you will be better familiar with what to cook for me while you tend the kitchen."

Gretchen nodded and asked Sadie, the cook I was fond of, for a quiet room that would be sterile and appropriate for us three. Sadie nodded and took us to her quarters that were kept clean and used only when she wasn't staying with her husband because of the kitchen's needs. The room was quaint and private. I had had no sort of examination like I was about to, but I put my body in the hands of Gretchen and Sadie. Both women helped me to undress, and because they were friendly and gentle, the awkwardness didn't affect me as much as it might have had it been someone else.

"Lay down, sweet Anne. It will be all right. It might be a little awkward, as this is your first time with such things, but we have done this, many times, and understand the fear of having this done for the first time. Just relax as much as you can, and breathe." Sadie had such a sweet and gentle voice when she helped me lie down.

Gretchen's hands moved around my belly and sometimes I giggled, though I tried hard to lie still. Sadie comforted me by holding my hand. Then Gretchen moved to the lower half of my body. She told me to take a deep breath while she tried to determine how far along I was. It was most uncomfortable, but I knew it must be important, for both me and the child. I knew I hadn't bled in several months, but

I didn't track this information at all. I was so wrapped up in writing to Henry, receiving his letters and small gifts, as well as writing to both Mary and Elizabeth. I also was fond of young Edward, but he was on a different path than that of the princesses, and so my time with him was very rare.

Gretchen had Sadie help me up, and both ladies helped me to dress. Smiling must've meant good news.

Gretchen said, "Anne, you are in your second term, nearing the end of that. It seems you are about five months along or so. How have you been feeling?"

I felt comfortable talking with her, so I told her I'd been feeling rather full of energy. My ladies-in-waiting, of course, knew of my condition, and I told her the father did not know, but I would somehow seek the energy to tell him one day. But I didn't want anyone else to know. This baby was all I had in the world next to my dearest household, and I didn't have the heart to go home to my brother and mother. I missed them, but not as much as I would miss England and her people. I was sure Gretchen wanted to know, but didn't dare ask who the father was. But I thought I could trust her.

"Gretchen, my secret must stay a secret, so the name of the baby's father must not leave your lips. For I do not want to disrupt his life, and I know he doesn't wish to marry me. The father is the king. Henry was here in December, and while he was here, we laughed and played games many nights, but he also stayed with me every night he was here. He was the only man I have ever shared a bed with. But he suffers so much, and he's not the man that people gossip about who don't know him. He's kind, and full of fun and laughter. Just, how do you say, misunderstood."

Gretchen looked at me and then at Sadie, where Sadie nodded to confirm what I just spoke. Gretchen seemed to understand and offered me a hug and her assurance that all would be well.

"Sadie, when do you depart, so transferring the cooking can take place with no change to the meal servings for the household? Also, given how much we know of her pregnancy, we need to add certain herbs to her diet to offer comfort rather than discomfort."

Sadie said she planned to leave with Little John tomorrow, as the boy was so excited to see the king and play games again.

The three of us then returned to the kitchen to find Lady Jane and Lady Mary looking for me.

Lady Katharine looked at me and scolded me to rest and take a nap, in my condition. I bade Gretchen and Sadie farewell for now, but not before telling them I needed to see them later.

I let Lady Katharine lead me to my room and dress me for bed. I was rather tired, and I felt faint. She touched my forehead, and it must have felt warm to the touch because I could hear her bellowing for cool clothes, and she hastened me to bed, propped against pillows and the windows open, though the air was rather hot. My belly cramped, and I wasn't sure what was going on. I wondered if this resulted from the examination, but other women went through this all the time. Was there something wrong with the baby? I showed some fear, I presumed, as my ladies started bothering about my health. I reminded them I was no longer queen, and no fuss should be made.

Lady Jane cut in and told me, "My lady, queen or not, queen matters not. You are the King's Beloved Sister, and a lady we all are fond of. Let us care for you. We'll keep your secret, but we know whose child this is. We must protect you and the baby."

"Send Gretchen here to help you. She's a midwife. And she knows."

Hours later the pain subsided, and I could rest easy. I knew I napped some, as when I awoke, I saw Gretchen tending to me with Lady Eleanor. I asked them what all happened and for them to tell me the truth. I wanted to know if the baby was still alive in me or if I had failed it already.

Gretchen sat on my bed and stroked the hair from my face. Her smile made me feel at ease. She told me that everything was going to be fine. My body must not have liked something I ate, and the body did what it could to protect the pregnancy.

"Sweet Anne, from this point on, I will oversee what you eat and drink until the baby is placed in your arms. Sometimes our bodies send us a message that we need to stop doing something it doesn't like. Like when men drink too much ale and they don't want to stop—well, their body makes them stop by forcing their stomachs to be empty, if you know what I mean. It's little things like that. You might have eaten something or overtired yourself. But I assure you, the baby and you will be fine if you rest and leave me in charge of the kitchen and your well-being. I will instruct your ladies on what you need to avoid for now to keep you comfortable and safe. With your permission, of course."

"Of course, Gretchen. Ladies Katharine, Eleanor, and

Jane will obey your instructions. I will, too. But do you think I can have some more bread? I love Sadie's bread."

She nodded and went to get me some.

Chapter Nine

Impulses — May 1542
Henry

I sat in my rooms trying to stay away from the constant urges of my council, wanting to know my intentions now that it had been three months since Catherine met her executioner. There were days I regretted knowing about her infidelity and treacherous past, and then there were days where I missed her vivacious youth and young firm body. I was growing older, and I knew it. I just didn't want to admit it. I sought Charles's advice, and as a loyal friend, he provided it. It was like he said. "We were once boys with the world at our feet and our thoughts to manifest change in the world, but as we get older, we must take our place in the world and find a way for our legacies to be remembered." What would I be remembered as?

I took council in the church. God owed me some

answers, as I had served him mercilessly and done his will. Once my servants saw me leave the chambers, it was like the entire court was on me for impending decisions. But my heart wasn't in it right now. This was my fifth wife, but none were a more true wife than my sweet Jane. And how she finally fulfilled a duty that was stripped away from me by all the others, except Anne, my beloved sister. I had my heir to continue the Tudor legacy. And deep down, I had reconciled with both princesses. Each different in their own way, but my Elizabeth was so determined — like her mother, but there was a zest for learning that came from me. This I knew from my mother. As of late, my legs had not troubled me, but I knew that was temporary.

I took my leave, and was almost trampled by what looked like a running monkey wearing a suit of armor without the helmet. A small monkey, but he seemed to have a sheepish grin and a certain boyish charm I recognized. Before I knew it, this monkey barreled into the tapestry, tearing it from the ceiling, and seemed to have crashed ahead of me. I couldn't help but laugh. The sight of my young friend was invigorating. I approached him to help him up, and as I did, I saw what he was running from. My servants were chasing him, and from what it looked like, they were covered in flour and what seemed like honey. I helped my young friend up and showed him a secret passage to my rooms from where we were. Once we arrived, we both laughed so hard that my servants came knocking on the door.

Looking at each other as if we were caught doing something we shouldn't have, I shouted, "What is it? I am indisposed."

The voice on the other side replied, "Your Majesty, we are searching for the kitchen troublemaker. Not a thief, but he caused a bit of a commotion with some of the soldiers by pouring honey on them to make their suits of armor tight, and…well, sticky. We must find him."

"Well, there is no one else here with me. Now, go away."

I wiped off the flour as best I could and really inspected the boy. He stared back at me at first as if he didn't know me, but then he laughed and put his arms around me.

Little John said, "I knew I'd find you. Can I call you Harry like before, or do I have to be grown up and call you 'king'? Mama said I need to mind my manners while we are here, and to serve you if you allow me to."

I was confused. Was Anne here? Did she come for a visit and I did not know it? Why wasn't I told? Someone's head was going to roll for this error.

I tussled Little John's hair. "Who all came with you? And, no, don't call me king. We are knights, you and I. You can call me Harry anytime you like. I prefer it over Henry at times. Is Lady Anne here, too? Where's your mother?"

"Mama is in the kitchen because she's going to be your cook for a while. It's a gift from Lady Anne so Mama can make those sweet breads you liked when you came over."

I quickly covered his mouth so he wouldn't blurt out where Charles and I were months ago. Though it was just the two of us in the room, I wanted him to know, not to mention it to anyone. I told him nicely that it was our little secret, but I wanted to know more about this surprise that was given to me. He changed the subject, asking if we could play. I looked at him, and he reminded me so much of my sweet Edward. In a little more than a year, my sweet Edward would begin his formal education and training to be my successor, and this would be more important than a father's indulgence to play games with his only son, as his only son was heir to the realm. But this boy, this Little John, was free from that, and perhaps I could spend some playful moments with him. Looking around my room, I tried to see what mischief we could get into. But as luck would have it, my servants had cleaned my room so that we couldn't even make the tiniest of messes.

Then I had an idea. I whispered to Little John, "Shall we be explorers and see what's in my tunnels?"

His face lit up, and I grabbed a torch, knowing we didn't really need it, but it made the effect more fun and real.

Moving the dark green tapestry and pushing open the secret door in the wall, I led the way for Little John and me to explore. Deep down I was giddy, as if I were a carefree young lad once more. Of course, my pace was slower now, and I was not in the same shape, but we managed just fine. As I led the way, I could hear Little John's "oohs and ahhs," as he was certainly excited. A rodent crossed our path and Little John stepped in front of me with his wooden sword. He pretended to do battle to defend his king.

"Well done, Sir Little John. You are going to make a fine knight in my guard, if your parents will agree. What say you?"

Little John stopped and knelt the best he knew how before me. "It would be my honor. I think Mama will say yes, but she worries when I even get a cut from playing with the chickens." He giggled even more.

Sometimes I wished the duties of king and being an heir to the throne wouldn't hinder the time I wanted to spend with my boy. But as he was the realm's most precious jewel and the only true heir to my throne, we must obey such protocol. I knew his mother, my lovely Jane, and I had talked about it so many times before he was born, but I missed this part. My father, bless his soul, was so duty bound because he'd fought for the throne that my mother made sure she was always attentive. But a woman's attention to a son was not enough.

Sighing deeply, I continued our journey. There were tunnels on each side of the pathway that I wasn't sure where they would lead. I knew how to get to the queen's chambers by going straight, but I thought we would try the left tunnel to see where it would go. There were no torches hanging on the walls, so I was glad I brought this torch. The air was dense, but periodically I would check on the boy.

"Are you all right, my young knight to be?"

"Yes, Majesty. It's scary though, but I'm brave. I can protect you."

Ruffling through his hair, I laughed, and of course thanked my newest knight. As we continued to walk down this tunnel path, eventually we came across something in our way. I held the torch closer to the ground to see what it was. Once I saw a skeleton, I tried to shield Little John from it, but he had already seen it. He didn't scare easily, and that was a good sign for a future knight. Before we could really explore the skeleton or go further into the tunnel, I thought I heard my men shouting. We weren't far into the tunnels and still close enough to my chambers. I motioned for silence so I could listen.

Then I heard it—my servants calling for the guards because I was missing. I was disappointed, but I knew we would have to turn back to avoid the commotion. Little John was as disappointed as I was, but we decided we would have to do this again. We hurried back to my room, where we were confronted by guards and my servants.

"Your Majesty, we found you. We thought something had happened to your person, and we were alarmed for your safety. What were you doing, and with this ragamuffin?" My guard was staring hard at the little boy, and I shielded him close to me to signify he had my protection.

"Damn fools. I was merely training my future knight, and I already told you I was indisposed this afternoon. Are you all daft?" I said in a very loud and commanding tone.

"Er, no, Your Majesty. I beg forgiveness. I was told you were missing. Isn't this the boy who caused a bit of a stir earlier when I was chasing him?"

"You are mistaken. His mother is serving as my cook, on loan from Anne of Cleves. Perhaps we will enjoy sweet cakes later today. This is her son, Little John. He has become as dear to me as Anne of Cleves, and is to be a future knight in my royal guard."

Turning to Little John, I bent over as much as my knees would allow me to. "Would you like to learn how to be a proper knight while you are here, if it is okay with your mother? I don't think my future knight should do any chores that will interfere with his training."

His eyes lit up, and he gave me the tightest hug his little arms could manage.

To my guard, I instructed, "See to his training while I speak to his mother. He will need a proper armor for his size and all. I place him in your care and expect that the same care and respect be given to him as my Edward. I believe he is five years of age. You never know, he might replace you one day when you can no longer hold a sword. He saved me from a foul creature scurrying in the tunnels. It was frightening!"

Little John looked at my guards and told them proudly, "It was an enormous rat, and he was scary."

The guards laughed, but remembered their obedience and quickly caught themselves and returned to position. I joined in the laughter and told them all was well. Releasing Little John to my guards, I promised we would play later. Everyone left my rooms save a council member. Looking at Thomas Audley, I put my hand on his shoulder and insisted he tell me what was wrong.

"Sire, are you sure about this boy? You know playing favorites with children of servants is highly improper. But we need your attention on court matters. It is a matter of—how should I say delicately—the choosing of Your Majesty's next wife."

I hung my head and told him we would discuss matters later. I must go speak to the cook about her son and find out exactly why I was given this most special gift if Anne did not come along. Thomas Audley departed, but not before reminding me of my duties and our continuing of the conversation. My thoughts ran all over the place once more, but I had promised the boy to seek his mother's permission. I began my walk to the kitchens, and eventually found myself with my royal party that usually accompanied me around the castle. While walking, I could get caught up with court affairs, and once more, the question came about regarding a betrothal for Edward. Luckily, I reached the kitchen before having to provide an answer.

"Madame Cook! I hear you are my special gift for a while. Tell me how this came to be!"

"Sire, it is kind of you to be joyous in welcoming me. My lady, Anne of Cleves, thought you would be honored with this surprise. I have special instructions, however, to ensure that I provide you my sweet breads, pigeon dishes, and the wonderful truffles you enjoy so much. How can I be of service to you now? It will be awhile before the breads are ready."

I smiled and said, "Please, do not bother so much. I am truly humbled and honored by this gift, and look forward to the wonderful foods you will prepare for me. However, I have an urgent matter of importance to discuss with you. Your son, Little John. I ran into him earlier—"

"Oh, Majesty. I apologize if he disturbed you. He's only five and doesn't know better."

"No, it is nothing like that. While you both are my guests, I would like to have him begin his training with my knights and guards. He has the makings of a fine knight in the future, and I would be honored to have him in my service. But I must request your permission."

Sadie's eyes widened, and she felt so humbled. With a curtsy, she answered, "Yes, Your Majesty. It would be my pleasure to have him train and learn how to be in your service. I am honored."

"It is I who am honored. But, as you are my guest cook, I will have your room prepared for you and Little John. He will be returned to you each night. But I must speak with you in private. Everyone else, leave me now."

Sadie shifted but was quite approachable as I sat on a stool. I needed to be off my feet, and could feel the puss again oozing through the flesh. Ignoring the slight pain for now, I asked Sadie for the truth of Anne, and how my former wife was doing.

"Sire, I am sworn to secrecy, but I can't lie to Your Majesty, either. My lady is well given her condition. She is happy and excited, and wanted me to provide you with the most delicious dishes that would brighten your days at this time. She understands the hardships you have endured and wishes only for your happiness and health. Asking nothing in return."

"Condition? Is she ill? Tell me."

Sadie breathed in and out heavily. "Sire, she is with a child."

I could feel the heat in my cheeks rise and my pulse quicken. I did not want to hear this, and I knew women wanted to have children, as it was their nature and purpose, but my Anne? Who was this man that got her pregnant with a child? Why didn't she tell me since I visited her before?

She must have noticed my cheeks having turned red and my temper growing because she put her hand on my hand and told me the rest. By the time she was finished, my answer was straightforward. I was the father of Anne's child. I sat down in disbelief, but Sadie assured me that Anne was content, healthy, and did not want to ruin her reputation and mine. It had been a safely guarded secret in her household, but I had so many questions I eventually overwhelmed the woman. I knew Anne well enough to know she was no harlot. A child of mine…a secret child. Deep down, I knew my council must never know about this child. I did not want Edward to feel his throne would be threatened by another sibling.

Sadie continued to tell me of Anne's health before one of my councilmen came running into the kitchen.

"Your Grace, here you are. We have called an emergency meeting of the council. You must attend now."

"What is the urgent nature of this meeting? Tell me now, good man."

The man shifted uneasily and looked at Sadie. I dismissed his look and demanded that he tell me, assuring him that anything he needed to tell me was safe in front of Sadie.

"Your Grace, a messenger arrived from the borders between here and Scotland. King James V, your nephew, has really taken sides with France. Ever since your sister, dear Margaret, passed, the tensions keep mounting between Scotland and England. It's almost as if King James V blames Your Majesty for his mother's unfortunate situation. We need you to review matters privately with the council. Make haste!"

I let Sadie know we would continue our discussion later, as I had more to know and needed her sweet breads. She nodded and returned to the kitchen work.

Chapter Ten

Motherhood — July 1542
Anne

Walking through the gardens provided me great happiness, and I knew the tradition of women being placed in confinement before giving birth, but I didn't wish to be locked up. Instructions were given to my ladies that I would remain free and about until the baby was born. I earned this freedom that I cherished from Henry. Many letters came from Henry these last few months, and a letter from Sadie. She and Little John were both in excellent health, and all were safe. That was our secret code to reassure me that Henry was unaware of the baby, which was what I wanted. I did not want to burden him with such news or for me to feel like one of the other women who bore him a child. Sadie's letter made me the happiest. She and Little John were going to be returning home once Little John finished his knight training. The king had kept him occupied with learning how to be a knight, and Sadie had the kitchens well stocked with Henry's favorite foods for long after her departure. I'd kept her letter, with one of Henry's latest, in my pocket because they made me the happiest. Henry wrote that while his leg ailed him from time to time, he was realizing it was going to be a hard summer. He didn't look forward to upcoming matters of state involving James V, his own nephew, but it was needed to show them the glory and might of England and her people. But with this letter, he also had included another locket, this time with a picture of just him on one side and the other empty. Would he think I would put a picture of me in it? What if I had a picture of the baby in it and kept the locket near my heart? Did he know about the baby?

As I continued to walk, an intense cramping gripped me, almost making me fall to the earth. Hunching over with one hand clasping my belly, I called for my ladies. At one point, the pain was so unbearable until I felt my water break. The baby was coming! Before I knew it, my ladies hurried me back inside and towards the birthing room that had been set up. Time seemed to drag on, and through my tears and screams, I heard my ladies telling me to bear down, push, and even to bite on a strap of leather. Lady Jane wiped down my forehead, reassuring me it would just be a few more pushes and to push a tad harder. The pain was excruciating as it continued for what I thought to be an eternity.

My ladies-in-waiting called for Gretchen, as Lady Katherine explained to me that the baby was struggling to come forth. I was relieved to have her with me. We'd had many talks about what to expect, but words could not prepare a woman for the actual event. Gretchen instructed my ladies, and told them that after hours of not delivering, I needed the birthing chair. Women were rushing about, and I could feel some of my ladies helping me towards the chair. It was a struggle between contractions, but Gretchen just reassured me that this was all normal. Women were built this way. This day was becoming longer and longer, and all I wished was for this to be over. Through the tears and pain, it was nighttime by the time she arrived. I could hear her cries as the ladies tended to her, but then another contraction ripped through me. This one was so fierce, and I yelled for Gretchen.

Gretchen checked me and instructed me to bear down.

"There's another baby. You are going to have to be strong. Bear down. Bite on the leather. Now push!"

Never in our talks did she mention there would be more than one, but she assured me she had known since that first day, but said nothing of twins that might cause me undue stress. Within minutes, a boy was born. Lady Mary took charge of the new baby and had him immediately swaddled and put next to his sister. I was exhausted and almost fainted. Gretchen told me that my choices were to either nurse them myself or have her seek a wet nurse, but discretion must follow given who the father was. Only those in the room closest to me knew the truth.

"I will nurse them myself. I want to be a true mother to them in every way, but I don't know what to do. Will you help me, Gretchen?"

One of my ladies brought me my baby girl. She had a reddish patch of hair and her features, though still new, were identical to Henry. The baby was a striking image of her father. There was also an uncanny resemblance to Elizabeth. "I will call her Margaret." Gretchen showed me how to have her latch onto me so I could feed her. When Margaret had her fill, Lady Jane took her, and then my son was placed in my arms.

"It's unmistakable. They both look exactly like Henry. How can I keep this a secret? Same hair coloring, same cheeks. Their features make them look like a miniature Henry. But he needs a name. A good name. I will call him John Wilhelm, after my father and brother. He looks strong."

Gretchen looked down at the boy and smiled. "Don't worry, Anne. Your children will be safe, and none will be the wiser. Feed him, and then you must rest. Childbirth is not an effortless task, and we will all be here when you wake. We will help you, won't we, ladies?"

I could hear them all agree, and was so thankful for my ladies. While he was nursing, I reflected on my ladies and how much I tried to show them I had grown to love them. I always remembered them through special gifts and all. We would raise my children in secrecy from knowing their parentage until they were much older to understand. I looked forward to seeing them grow up, and as I thought happily about this, I fell asleep.

Later, I awoke to find Gretchen bringing me one baby to nurse and then the other. In addition, a bowl of broth was waiting for me. She told me how important my nourishment was to feed the babies, as well as my rest. I had news that the childbirth, though painful, was a healthy one, and that I should stay in my post birth confinement. The household was functioning properly, and Lady Mary had informed some of the townspeople that I had come down with a simple stomach bug, but would be around before they knew it.

While I remained in confinement, I received periodic letters from Henry. This recent letter was most alarming to me, for I knew he wanted to keep his vigor and health, but an upcoming battle he was planning would not allow him to. He wrote to tell me to stay safe and protect the lands while his army marched to Scotland to show King James V the power and might of beautiful England. Henry said I should not worry about his safety, but to please pray for the lives of his army so God would bless them and bring them to victory. He offered no details, but also told me he planned on another secret visit at some point.

One of my ladies sat near me, watching over the babies and keeping me company. Lady Jane looked over to me and asked if the king had anything special to say. I told her he would be arriving one day soon, like he had done in secret many times before, and that he was preparing for a battle against Scotland. Her eyes showed a little fear, and quickly she made the sign of the cross and clasped her breast in prayer. "We will all pray for them, Lady Jane."

I endured the confinement, and we called for a priest we could trust with news of the condition, etc. He came on the last day and blessed me, so I could return to running my household. Though highly unusual, he provided a secret baptism for the twins so they would be children of God. He took one look at them and then looked at me, with an eyebrow raised in suspicion.

"Lady, I do not mean to speak out of turn, but I must ask. The resemblance is uncanny, and the twins look remarkably like the king. I know you are His Majesty's most beloved sister, and all respect is shown to you save his daughters and the queen—when we have one again? How do you plan to keep this revelation from His Majesty? It is his bloodline, after all."

We looked at him and I felt scared. Could I not bring the twins out to town? What if I wanted to move to another one of my castles? What should I do? I really did not think so far ahead about all this. In fact, I did not think I would have gotten pregnant, but Henry was just so captivating last December.

The priest put his hands on my shoulders. "Child, it is all right. It was the will of the king. But with his moods and lack of male heirs, if anything were to happen to Edward, you must guard the boy at all costs. I will document this, but keep the parchment hidden. When the time comes for the king to know, you and I will tell him. In the meantime, have you thought about his upbringing at all? He's a baby now, but in time, he will be a young boy. The king was educated in the ways of the church because of his lady grandmother, but that changed when Arthur passed. You could bring him up similarly, but prepare him with more worldly knowledge, too. When you have decided, send for me. As for the girl, raise her similarly to the Princess Elizabeth. The Tudor Dynasty must be protected."

"Aye, Father. I will do as you instruct. Let me think of the boy, and one of my ladies will send for you when the time comes. But you are right, King Henry will have to know, but I can do that on my own. I will tell him of your gracious help so as not to disturb Edward's line of succession, but I understand the need for heirs. I have learned a lot since coming to England. My lady will show you out, as I must tend to the children."

While nursing the babes, I wondered how I was going to tell Henry the news, and feared he would be displeased by the unexpected burden. I had to come up with something. It's not like I could bring them there in front of the entire court. Heaven forbid! Such a thought would unsettle everyone. Remembering Henry's letter, I thought maybe he would come here sooner than expected. But how to raise the boy? He was the most important, but I loved the idea of having my own children. Lady Mary was quite an adult already and needing a husband, while Lady Elizabeth was just a vivacious child, full of life and with a strong sense of intelligence like her father.

Margaret was a calm eater, and she fussed so little. She ate and then fell asleep. She was such a calm baby. Swaddled and full, I had returned her to her cradle before turning my attention to John Wilhelm. He had what I thought of as a bit more of a temperament and took his time feeding. He had a tuft of reddish hair, and his small, beady eyes reminded me of a miniature Henry. He didn't fall asleep right after, so I took this extra time with him, thinking about his future.

"Sweet little one, you have a future of possibilities ahead of you. You are the king's son, though illegitimate, I suppose, but blood is blood if I ever knew it. Shall you succeed somewhere in line to the throne after Edward, or another? Or shall we raise you in the eyes of the Church? Your father will recognize you in an instant, but I hope he will at least claim you and your sister. But neither of you could disrupt the line of succession.

John Wilhelm must have not liked my open thoughts because he started crying, and no matter how hard I tried, he would not stop until I laid him next to his sister. Once together, he fell asleep, safe and content.

Chapter Eleven

The Battle of Haddon Rig—August 1542
Henry

I had listened so many times to my council tell me of my nephew James's alliance with France that the anger and rage seethed through to my fist as I slammed it on the table. The room became silent as they heard the loud bang, commanding silence. "Enough! I've had it with my nephew. Despite being my sister Margaret's boy and heir to Scotland, I demand a respite! I am the king of England. Why must the Northern borders continue to suffer from these attacks? We must have justice."

Some of my council seemed uneasy at this thought, while the others longed for a battle against the Scots and their inconceivable alliance with France.

"Your Majesty, if I may. Since Francis I is distracted with his Holy Roman Emperor Charles V, he does not seem all that interested in Scotland at the moment. Since your nephew has the maddening balls to reject you and continue to show favor to France, this might be an opportunity to, how should we say, show those Scots the pure might and glory of England. Of course, I am sure this is what you meant by showing us your rage just now, am I right?" questioned Thomas Audley.

I thought for a moment on his words, and he must have read my mind about how to get a respite from King James V. I must reward him for his loyalty, but I wondered how things were with his wife. Their daughter must be around two now. As I thought more about his wife, my member came alive and I needed relief. Putting that aside, I knew I must act according to my conscience and to what the council suggested.

I rubbed my hand across my beard, immersed in the serious thought of going to war. It had been some time since we had a good bloody battle, but I knew as much as I wanted to be part of it, I couldn't. I didn't know if this upset me more, or the pain that had just shot through my leg.

"Have the Duke of Norfolk take men and protect the border. They must seek to guard the realm and protect it at all costs, and if a skirmish occurs in which they can take an advance against Scotland, do so. Win me Scotland as soon as possible."

Sir Audley and Sir Gage were on my side, while there were a few that did not seem taken with the idea of another skirmish with the Scots. I knew I couldn't truly voice my inner feelings to the council, but I felt sorry at the idea of taking retribution on my sister's son. Yet I couldn't let him continue to favor France when I was kin and king of England. And then he had married Francis's daughter, of all things. More

French nonsense that he was favoring. What a foolish boy.

I waited for what seemed like an eternity, although I knew it was only days since sending my men out. Every day I would ask the Privy Council if they'd heard word from the Duke of Norfolk or Sir Robert Bowes, one man tasked with invading Scotland while the duke guarded the borders. Finally, a messenger came running through the gates. I saw him enter from the window and immediately tried to reach him, but as my leg was giving me some ghastly trouble, he reached me in minutes.

Panting, he dropped to his knee with his head bowed.

"Rise and tell me what news you bring me. Did we have a victory?"

Turning to one servant, I ordered food and a drink for him, hoping this would make the words fall out of his mouth faster than the silence I was receiving now.

"Sire, Sir Robert Bowes had an opportunity and aided with the Earl of Angus. They slipped into the realm of Kelso, where they split into different armies. We moved toward about two or three settlements, and before we knew it, the Scots had advanced from Kelso and from another direction. It seemed like we were surrounded, and all bloody hell broke out. The rear of our army was struck by the Scots, while the front endured bloodshed. Before we knew it, Sir Bowes couldn't maintain control. The Scots easily overtook us, and all was lost. About a thousand men were taken. Sir Robert Bowes was one of them. The Scots had spies that knew of our plans, and—well, if I can be bold to Your Majesty, Sir Bowes lost control and couldn't get his head straight to figure out how to give Your Majesty a well-earned victory."

The heat in my face warmed my cheeks and my breathing became shallower and deeper. I was beyond rage and anger. "Bring me my Privy Council now. Thank you, good man. Eat and drink and rest. I wish the news was different."

I saw my council running toward me with haste. It was about damn time. Turning to join them, we made our way to the council chambers. While we walked there, I told them what was relayed to me. As they sat, I leaned over the table and looked them dead in the eye. "How did we fail? What was that imbecile thinking? I heard the report from the messenger himself."

Sir William Petre somberly stated the truth. "I believe Sir Bowes acted in haste, and now we don't even know if he remains alive or dead in the hands of the Scots, along with the other men. Your Grace, we must plan a second attack, but one with more strategy and secrecy. I believe if we do this and with our resources, we can make Scotland fall to their knees. You know we've done it once before with King James IV, his father. We just need your encouragement to prevail, and a formidable army that won't be easily fooled. We can exploit their weakness, leaving Scotland vulnerable, and perhaps combined, we can invade France at some point. But we sever that alliance between Scotland and France while we have a chance."

Sir John Gage stood and said it would be foolish to try so soon. We must wait. Then all I heard was bickering between my council. Before we could continue, the doors opened loudly, and a page came running through with a message in his hands.

"I have a message for the king! It is from Lord Huntly,

the leader who captured Sir Bowes and others."

Ripping it from his hands, I tore it open and read it aloud.

"I, Sir Huntly, have captured a thousand of your men who thought they could invade Scotland. But it is I who approached them on Haddon Rig and fought to victory. All in the name of Scotland and King James V. Among them are your commanders. You will hear from King James V when it is time."

I screamed, tearing the parchment to shreds. "Bring the best commanders in my army to me. They will sit here with the council and plan a strategy that will be decisive." The messenger rushed out of the room to heed my instructions.

Holding a shredded piece in my fist, I banged it needlessly on the table, but I wanted my council to understand that this loss would not go unpunished. The damn fool of Norfolk, not a duke at this loss, cost me a significant win. But I felt we could overturn this defeat and conquer Scotland. But how? Silently, I knew my men could use me in battle, but my body no longer heeded the cry for war. The pain in my legs saw to that, but my chief physicians could not find a curable remedy for this tortured body. Again, was it my punishment from God? How much more did I need to bear when I served Him? My mind floated at the thought of Anne and how I missed being able to confide in her about things, but I knew my focus was here and now, not on her.

Before I could shout further at my council for this loss, a soldier from my army came in and knelt before me. I looked closely at him and gave him a rise. Transforming the English army took a military mind, like mine, and I recognized this man. I trained him when he was younger. I knew him to be capable, and therefore I smiled.

"Rise. Work with us, my good man. Help this foolish council devise a plan that would surely put Scotland on its arse and bowing to England, if you know what I mean."

My soldier requested to speak freely, and by all means, it was granted and more. I called for ale, cheese, breads, grapes, and more to be brought.

"If you can guarantee me retribution for this loss, I will grant you anything. Just bring me victory. Bring your king his due glory."

The soldier nodded and looked at the table and the council before he spoke. He made sure he knew exactly to whom he would be speaking. While he did so, he placed his hand around his neck, as if to protect it.

"I will not cut your head off, fool. I need a plan. I need a sound plan to win. Can you give me one?"

He made himself comfortable at the table and pulled the map closer to him. He studied the border and the different villages that were already marked as likely places.

"Sire, this will take time, but I think I know how you could flush King James V out of his 'hidey hole.' I would propose that we send a moderate size army—not too small but not too large. Their goal would be to just burn the villages right over the border, just the right amount to get his attention. I'm bloodthirsty as I think this aloud, but if you burn the villages, animals, everything, he will come out. But if you leave people alive, he won't take you seriously. You must bully him into coming back to us. If he comes toward us, we will be ready with more forces. But you must call him out.

Now, if I can plainly speak — you can't put the same soldiers back in battle. They are not prepared to do what is needed. You need bloodthirsty soldiers. You need a bloodthirsty army to defeat the Scots."

I pondered his suggestion. I nodded for him to tell me more.

"My king, a bloodthirsty soldier does not care about the woman standing in front of him in a battle. It sounds harsh, as much as I love my wife, but she knows that my first duty is to protect and fight for my king. She would call me a weakling if I let a woman standing in front of me in a battle be spared. I am a brute. My life is to secure your throne and to gain the victories for you. If I can't — well, let's just say my wife would eat my balls for supper. If you know what I mean."

Slapping him on the back, I knew what he meant. I knew he would be the man for this. But I had questions to his plan and asked him to think about the second part — what to do when King James V came out of his hidey hole?

My man thought long and hard, and grabbed the map from the council. He made a circle and said aloud, "Sirs, if we plant ourselves here and are not seen, we can send a small group to invade here," pointing to another area. "Then if we allow them to have their Scottish hearts fill with pride in hopes of another victory, one army can circle them from here while another from this point." He pointed to the various sides on which my army could capture the Scots in a most decisive victory.

I was seeing his cunning and strength. I wondered if I may have overlooked his worth in my army as I listened to his plan, falling on every word.

"Once the hearts of these Scottish fools think they have us beat, I estimate that—for example, if I were leading this group, I could sweep over here and take the head off the dragon! I believe this would be the more likely place in which King James V would lead from. The man wants to be part of the action, but is too feeble to lead without a significant wall of men in front of him. In considering all possibilities, I expect a greater loss on the side of the Scots than with our men, but we must choose the men wisely. I have no desire to repeat this last battle that ended up with most of us dead or captured."

I slapped my soldier on the back with my right hand and handed him a glass of ale.

"Tell me, soldier, do you command where your men obey you? I see great things in you, and yet you haven't told me your name. Why keep me guessing?"

"I am Thomas Warton, Your Majesty. My men obey with no objection, but I have gone many nights giving those in whom I saw promise extra training. I believe this plan will work if you give me the chance to lead it. I must pick the men that will give you what you seek most in this against the Scots."

"Tell me more about this plan. My council and I will give you what you seek."

And we began planning the response after the failure of Haddon Rig.

Chapter Twelve

Sleepless Nights — November 1542
Anne

I lay in bed, tossing and turning. Part of me longed for Henry to be there, and part of me just enjoyed being a mother. So many things to learn and so many questions regarding the little babies. Each month, they grew to look more and more like Henry. I wished I could tell him, but that would jeopardize his crown and his heart after so many losses. As much as I wanted to reunite with Henry, I knew he didn't have the same desire. Being his "Beloved Sister" was more gracious, and I knew I secretly held his heart as much as he had mine. Letters had come from Henry these last few months, and he told me of a battle loss in August that left him defeated until a new plan was devised. My response to him was that he was the greatest king of England, and his people loved him, win or lose, but I would pray for a glorious victory that would seal his place in history.

Everything was as nice as expected here with my household and my babies. Most of all, I was happy though my heart ached, and I missed seeing Princess Elizabeth, but she wrote to me often and was so busy with her studies. Her father visited her almost every day to see how she progressed, but she wanted to come see me. As I read that letter, I remembered the gift her mother had left her. I wondered how old she should be before I shared this with her. Maybe just a few more years. I was constantly lost in my thoughts. Perhaps that was why I was not sleeping and I lay awake at night, listening to the flames while the babies slept.

I must've fallen into a deep sleep because my ladies woke me and motioned for me to get ready. They seemed to be in quite a state, with all the bustling they had done. I rushed through the usual protocols of getting dressed and with taking care of the babies, and finally caught my breath to ask my lady about the state of hurriedness.

Lady Katharine said, "You have a visitor in the inner hall, and we needed the babies to be fed so you won't be rushed. He is from King Henry's court with a message for your eyes only. You must think about letting one of us find you a nurse for the twins so we can keep them safe from prying eyes. Let me have Lady Jane finish your corset while I bring the babies to you."

While Lady Jane finished getting me dressed, Lady Katharine held the babies, one in each arm. Listening to them make their little noises filled my heart with great joy. As I watched them, Lady Katharine told me something that made me shiver. She explained a tale that was secretly passed from generation to generation. I listened to her words.

"Many years ago, King Philip IV, the king of France, burned and tortured the soldiers of God's army, The Knights Templar. Before he could get to torture and kill the last Templar Knight, the grand master, a curse was formed. The Grand Master, Jacques de Molay, died in what was called a death of injustice. But before he was burned, Jacques de Molay incited a curse that would last many years. What's important about this and the Templar Knights is that they were tortured unjustly for seven long years for crimes they never committed. These were the soldiers of God.

"Jacques de Molay and another templar called upon Christ to bring justice to the Templar Knights from King Philip IV's heinous judgement and behavior, as well as to the pope, who declared himself to be more supreme than the living and true God. They swore that there would be a reckoning in which King Philip IV would answer to the Lord Almighty God for these crimes against the loyal knights of God, in which each bloodline of King Philip IV would not survive for generations. In fact, shortly after the grand master died, it is said that the heavens opened, and a storm raged. Pope Clement died not long after, and it was soon followed by the death of King Philip IV. In fact, his male line died. God acknowledged the curse.

"Now, our good King Henry VIII is part of that line through King Philip's daughter, Isabella. Isabella was the great grandmother of our king's lady grandmother, Margaret Beaufort. I know this is a lot of history for you, but the result is this: supposedly, the line is cursed, and thus, no sons will live from King Henry's seed because of the grand master's curse. So, my lady, at some point, the young master here will not make it to continue the line. I don't want to alarm you, but felt you needed to know what the rumors are. This is a powerful curse because it is a request to God from one of his most humble and true servants, Jacques de Molay."

As I clung to every word she said, a single tear fell from my eye. My heart broke by the end of the story, and I had to ask her, "Is there any way to undo the curse? I don't want to lose John Wilhelm."

Lady Katharine took hold of my hand and put a finger to my lips. "You mustn't speak of curses so loudly. But Lady Jane and I can help you. That's why it's only the two of us tending to you this morning. The messenger downstairs must be dealt with first. Once you are done with that piece, we will begin, and need to call upon Gretchen to help us. Understand?"

I nodded and prepared to greet the messenger. As I made my way to the inner hall, I wondered what Lady Katharine could do. But once I recognized the messenger from Henry's personal service, I quickened my stride. As the messenger bowed, I replied with the customary curtsy, as this messenger was in Henry's personal circle, which was valued.

"Lady. I bring you a message from King Henry himself. He asked that I wait for your reply before returning to him," he said as he handed me the letter.

I read it, trying to make sure I didn't color my cheeks because of Henry's flattery. But as I read further, I sensed Henry was trying to allude that he knew about the babies, but he didn't come out and say that. Instead, he merely hinted that he would like to visit as soon as he could, and wondered about any changes in my current household. Once I finished, the messenger took a parcel out and handed it to me. It was a beautiful handkerchief with my coat of arms on it. I asked him to wait while I penned my response.

> *Dearest Henry,*
>
> *I was pleased to hear about your happiness in your army's planning, and look forward to the day on which you will be arriving. Everyone in my household is just thriving, and is as glorious with life here, as I am sure your own household is. Little John continues his training to this day so that one day, in your service, he will make you proud. My heart sends you the greatest of love and affection, and I will pray for Godspeed and your victory.*
>
> *Your loving and humble servant and sister,*
> *Anne*

I folded my letter and placed my seal on it. Giving it to the messenger, I told him to stop by the kitchen for some food and wine before returning to Henry. I didn't want to rush him, but I was most eager to return to my ladies.

I sprinted to my rooms and sought Lady Katharine. I begged her to tell me how to fix the curse, as John Wilhelm was from Henry's bloodline. She sent Lady Jane to find Gretchen and the others, some of whom I had never heard of before. As I waited, I held John Wilhelm in my arms while Margaret slept contently. She never gave me a fuss, but John Wilhelm was quite the one to demand attention. Lady Katharine told me of two ladies named Edith and Sara who would come to my aid.

After a short while, ladies filled my room, and once

they saw the babies, they gasped. These two were miniature versions of Henry. In fact, as much as Princess Elizabeth bore a strong resemblance to her father, these two were even more striking to match almost all of Henry's features. Edith, the older lady of the two, peered down closer to John Wilhelm, taking in his features. John Wilhelm was a remarkably handsome baby.

"My word! He is a miniature version of King Henry himself! I would know. I may be an old crone now, but I was one of the royal midwives to his late mother, Queen Elizabeth of York. She had a beautiful soul, and when she birthed Henry, I was there helping her. But looking at this wee little one, he is exactly like his father. There is no mistaking it. And this one here, his sister. The resemblance is there, as well as looking like King Henry's mother. They are Tudor children. No doubt about it. I assume, my lady Anne, you are their mother and not some common mistress because of the request of secrecy we were given?"

I looked at Lady Katharine, who gave me a slight nod. "Yes, ma'am. I am their mother, though I agreed to the marriage annulment with King Henry. But I do not wish for anything for myself but to save my son. I've always longed for children, no matter how naïve I may be to things. And I do not wish to dishonor the king, but we are all his subjects to obey his command." Putting a hand to my neck, Edith noticed that movement and nodded.

"Yes, we are all pawns to men. But let us help you. I assume Lady Katharine told you about the curse that was laid upon the bloodline and why."

I nodded.

"Good, then let's begin. Sarah, hold her hand and let's form a circle. Come now, ladies. This is not an easy curse to break because we can't ask God to break the curse for the pain and suffering of those Templars. We must ask for something, and in return, Lady Anne, you will need to agree to a sacrifice. We don't know what God will require, but if he finds your heart true, he may grant it for a price because the sins of King Philip IV and Pope Clement can't be forgiven easily. It was an injustice. Do you understand?"

Again, I nodded. I would do anything to save my son.

"It will cost you, dear child. But that price is between you and the Heavenly Father."

We formed a circle around the two cribs, holding hands. I listened to Edith chant in a language I had never heard before. But my heart told me to trust her and place all my being in God's hands. Closing my eyes, I swayed to the chanting. Then I felt a stinging in my wrist. Opening my eyes, I saw that someone had taken a dagger and made a tiny slit to draw blood. Edith grabbed my hand and let the blood drip onto the foreheads of both children. It had to be both because they were twins. I didn't scream or question because I gave her my complete trust. Something I had never given to Henry before. There was always something holding me back, but that wasn't a concern right now.

I nearly collapsed in the arms of another person.

"Someone fetch the water. She fainted," was all I heard before my eyes closed once more. This time, I was neither asleep nor awake. I must've been dreaming.

I was walking along the garden and I came across the most beautiful little bird I had ever seen. It was chirping, but it sounded like it was in pain. I picked up the little creature and cradled it in my handkerchief. I noticed the coloring was most unusual for a bird. It was a beautiful golden color with speckles of green and red in its feathers. I looked all around where I found it, but I saw nothing that could've injured it. Then I noticed he was trying to fly but couldn't. The little bird was scared, but it seemed to have settled once I brought him close to my eyes to look.

As I smiled at him to reassure him, I felt a warmth in my hands and heart. Instantly, his wings stretched as he remained in the palm of my hands. And I could feel a sense of love around me. In my mind, I heard a sound. "Daughter, I deliver unto you your children, to love and grow. In return, know that they will be loved, and find love, but the seed must stop with them. Be strong, daughter, for my grace is with thee."

As I felt the cool water on my forehead and felt the drops of water on my lips, I knew God spoke to me, and I would accept his will.

"Edith, Sara, God has granted the request. This I know. But I feel so tired. Would you mind if I just rested a while? Please guard my secret the best you can."

Edith and Sara looked at the children and then back at me. They nodded, for they must have known that the curse would keep them safe.

Chapter Thirteen

The Battle of Solway Moss — November 1542
Henry

My morning meal was interrupted with news of the attack. Every night since my capable soldier left to carry out his plans, I wondered if this time I could bring James to his knees. Though my nephew, he had become an arrogant bastard. I thought meaningfully this whole time about complete dominance over Scotland, and was hopeful. If my father could secure our Tudor throne and unite the two houses of Lancaster and York on a mere promise, then why couldn't I take control of Scotland on a promise? Or was I getting too soft in my old age?

"Come here, boy. Bring me the news. Did Thomas Walton bring his country's glory and pride? Are we pleased? I'm waiting!"

The messenger brought forth a letter, written by

Thomas Walton himself, but I saw the seal had not been broken. "Bring in my Privy Council. Now!"

As I waited for the Privy Council to make their attendance, I couldn't wait any longer. I took my knife and broke the seal. I glanced through it quickly to see if I could see the words my heart had hoped for, but then, as I squinted, I started back at the top.

> *My Lord King,*
>
> *I write this report to tell you about the events that took place on the evening of 23 November, in the year of our Lord, 1542. As I dined with my men, some spies I had sent forth to bring me word about the Scottish proved to be true. As we had raided earlier in the day, I expected to have retribution from them in order to flush out King James V. My spies told me they overheard the Scots planning an attack for the morrow.*
>
> *On 24 November, in the year of our Lord 1542, I gathered a few hundred men to lie in wait to watch over the River Esk. I couldn't believe my eyes when I saw that King James V had close to twenty thousand men crossing the river in the area known as Solway Moss and making their way into England. These men looked beaten, tired, and not prepared for war. The Scots were already beaten based on how they looked. I had some men watch the Scots try to retreat, because they saw our flags hoisted, and my Lord King, we made them think we were many. As they tried to retreat, I sent one group to attack from the left and the other from the rear. I will confess that these Scots have hearts like Englishmen, but sire, they do not have you for a king.*
>
> *As to the battle, I have secured the victory as my word given unto you. The unfortunate news is that King James V fled, but not*

before I could ensure a good licking with my English sword. He
will think twice next time for his cowardice should he face me. Your
victorious army, sire, has secured over one thousand prisoners. The
rest are dead by our hand or drowned because of the river. Your
army is powerful considering our small amount compared to theirs.

Enclosed is the coat of arms from a soldier in King James V's
army. Take this as a sign that I plucked it off the dead corpse of a
Scot for you alone.

I await further instructions from Your Majesty, but am
eager to return to court.

Your humble servant,

Thomas Walton

I looked at the tattered cloth of the dead Scot, smeared
with his dried blood, and clutched it hard in my hand as my
Privy Council entered the room.

"Majesty, we have come per your beckon."

"Lords, Thomas Walton did it! His plan worked, and
he brought us a most decisive victory to make up for the
blundering loss from before. We must call him home for a
celebration. Look, read his letter. That fool nephew of mine
went retreating home like a coward donkey. But he was
injured, it seems. A more detailed report can be given later
when we see him next at court."

"Your Grace, now is the time to secure this victory. We
think that King James V has suffered with this loss. We need
to secure the hold you have in Scotland. Isn't his wife due
any day now with a baby? If it's a girl, you might consider
an alliance with Prince Edward, because there is no way that
France is going to step in to assist Scotland right now. But we
must secure your hold."

I knew I would have to make an alliance somehow, and this seemed logical, but without knowing the identity of his heir, I couldn't make such a decision — at least not yet. But I knew Thomas Walton needed to be rewarded.

"Leave me. I want to finish my morning meal in peace."

As I finished eating, I wondered about Anne and the fact that there would be a child. Another chance for an heir if all else failed me, or if there was another punishment from God. As much as I was needed here, especially in the aftermath of Solway Moss, I made my trip to see her. I wanted to know the truth and to see Anne. But as my thoughts were getting carried away, the cardinal appeared.

"Your Majesty, we must talk about another queen. Surely you have given thought to some suitable royal ladies. Preferably one that will not dishonor Your Majesty," said the cardinal.

I was tired of his badgering about another queen. In the end, they had failed me, except for Queen Jane. She took to her death the same way my mother had. She was a true queen in every sense, and left me my most prized heir, Prince Edward. I made her a promise upon her deathbed. I would see to his care personally and ensure that no harm came to him. Even my Elizabeth had taken to him like a true sister should. I wondered, however, what would have happened if my Henry Fitzroy would have lived, too. The sorrow and grief weighed heavy on me.

Not wanting to deal with the cardinal today, I sent word to my master of the horse to prepare a strong and fast steed. I was going riding and would take a small envoy with me. As much as I liked grand gestures, I preferred the quieter approach when visiting Anne. I knew she was someone I could confide in, despite my initial displeasure at our marriage. I may have softened, but she was the only queen, other than Queen Jane, who understood and respected my nature.

I rode out with Charles, as he was the only one whose council I could trust regarding politics and my secret visits to Anne. I did not want these visits to be noticed for people thinking there would be another union. I had my appearances to maintain. As we rode, I took a chance and tell him news of Anne but that I wasn't supposed to know.

"Charles, you know how Sadie came to cook for me for a while as a gift from Anne?"

"Yes, Henry. She makes some fine sweet cakes. What's on your mind? Scotland or something else?"

"Sadie told me that Anne became with child since our last visit. She should have had her baby by now. She and I had relations, but I didn't think she would end up with a child. But Anne is concerned about her reputation, given her new title as my sister. I want no harm to come to her, nor do I want the cardinal or anyone else to know. She would become a tool in this wretched game, but I desire her happiness since she gave me mine with no argument. What do you think I should do?"

Chuckling, he said, "I'm the wrong person to seek council from on women. Look at how many wives I have had so far. I say this with the most respect to you, Henry – I loved Mary more than any other. I disrespected you when I married her in secret, and I will beg your forgiveness for all time. But your sister had an unexplained hold on my heart, and I gave her mine in return. So, Henry, I think you might be in love with Anne. I know we talked about it before, but I say it once more to you. You might have found your way to her heart finally, but you are king. You can marry her once more, or keep things as is and keep her close to your heart and away from the court politics.

"I say this as your brother, Henry. Be wary of those around you, especially in your Privy Council. There's something unusual about them. They shut me out long ago, but I have my spies to make sure you are well protected. They might already have decided on your next queen."

Laughing, I slapped him on the back as we continued riding onward. He began coughing, and I worried about him as our ages kept increasing while, I hated to admit, our virility went down.

"I'm all right Henry. It's just the season, and who knows what else."

Surveying the countryside, I noticed the land was changing because of the season. Soon, Christmas would be upon us, and it'd be time for another celebration. How to make the court cheerful with no queen? How could I make this festive for Prince Edward? The lad had no mother, but my Elizabeth filled that role. Maybe I should send them to visit Anne? Or bring Anne back to court somehow. Regardless, we were almost at her castle. Charles and I filled the remaining time laughing and reminiscing of our youth.

Chapter Fourteen

Family — November 1542
Anne

Henry and Charles were in the garden when my ladies came to announce their unexpected arrival. It was a surprise, and though I wasn't sure how I would handle it, my stomach tightened at the thought of the babies. I asked both Lady Katherine and Lady Jane to bring them with me as I greeted the men.

I received kisses on the cheek from both Henry and Charles, and just by looking at them, I could tell they knew. So, with my free hand, I motioned for my ladies to bring the children.

"Charles, Henry, I could tell you know my secret, but I beg you, please do not judge me harshly. For they are truly your children, Henry, but I ask nothing from you. In fact, please do not make them go to court. I want no ill between me and whoever your future queen will be."

Henry reached out for Margaret, lifting her from Lady Katharine. "There's two of them? I thought you had only one child. Two is quite the gift from God."

As he examined Margaret, I could tell he was overcome with emotion. Charles reached for John Wilhelm.

"I named them John Wilhelm, after my brother and father, and Margaret, after one of your sisters. To bring honor to your house and to you."

"They look like me. Look at their little eyes. And those cheekbones. In fact, they look like Lady Elizabeth. Charles, what do you think of these little heirs?"

I could tell Henry was proud and elated, but I reminded him I asked that they have a life outside of court, especially since every care in the world was being taken to secure Prince Edward's reign. Charles laughed and took hold of Margaret's chubby foot, and squeezed each of the little toes in a sign of affection. She squirmed with laughter in Henry's arms as Charles tried to maintain his hold with John Wilhelm in his while playing with Margaret.

My ladies brought refreshments and eventually took the babies back inside to the children's nursery. Henry kissed my cheek once more, and offered his most sincere promise that they would be left in my care without interruption from the court, but how he would like to very much be part of their lives as their father, not their king.

My heart felt such relief that I had to share something with Henry. I didn't plan on Charles being present, but I took the chance while I had it. I explained I had learned so much while living my life away from court, and how I got to know the different villagers and townsfolk.

"Henry, sit for this. I am not sure how much is true or a rumor, but I would like to save John Wilhelm at any cost. I am not good with the English language still, but it's getting better." And with that, I relayed the story of the Templar Knight curse and the fact that this could be the reason males did not live long through Henry's line of heirs. By the time I'd finished, I thought both men would be angry or call me foolish, but I simply received the words, "A reason that makes sense. This I could believe, and technically, I'm not to blame, but my blood is. Tell me, Anne, do you know more?"

Charles began coughing harder and looked pale. I called for one lady to show him to his room to rest, with instructions for broth to be sent to him. He was like a brother to me, considering how much he had helped me since I arrived in England, and I couldn't let anything happen to him.

After he left, I reached for Henry's hand to comfort him, and told him all I had learned. He listened as if he were the student and I the teacher. I knew Henry to be a man of intellect, and how he had an insatiable thirst for learning. I had hoped I could recall the version of the Templar Knight story exactly as it was told to me. As I had done so, Henry's eyes seemed to have drifted from me to books that lined the shelves of my bookcase. Pulling his hand away, he asked if he could look at these books.

"Some of these never left here when I took control of the castle after the Boleyns had fallen far from favor. I knew Sir Thomas Boleyn and other members of his family to be scholars. In fact, Anne Boleyn was a remarkable woman before she lost her head. I believe they might have a book here that could be part of the history. They were intrigued not only with life at court and the power that their daughters could bring them, but like everyone else, they wanted the truth behind the Tudor Dynasty. And Sir George Boleyn, my foul brother-in-law at one point, was a man who thirsted for knowledge, and had many items thought lost to history in his possession. My lady grandmother, the one that comes from the Beaufort line you mentioned, was always so strict and pious that I wonder if she even knew about this. I'm sure she probably did, but my father was not pleased with all her rules. People think I am a fool and lavish compared to my father's tightness with money and things, but I am not. I let them think that only because I don't know who to trust anymore.

"I wonder what other secrets Anne Boleyn has hidden from me. Being here makes me wonder, and I shouldn't. This is your home now. I had erased all memory of the Boleyns long before."

"Henry, don't be foolish. Let's look together. I am intrigued by this so-called curse and your family history, now that we have children. But I beseech you. Let me raise them here, away from court and gossip. Of course, you are welcome here anytime your heart finds its way. I give you my solemn word that no one will be the wiser as to their true identities, and I will not take offense when Edward succeeds you at the proper time. I do not wish to wed any man again, and seek only your happiness."

"Anne, let me be frank with you. I heard from your brother, and he seeks that I either send you back to Cleves or marry you once more to restore you properly. I sense your mother's input in his writing, but I did not wish to keep this secret from you. What say you?"

I looked at him plainly, just like I did during his last visit. "I have no interest in returning to become my brother's property again, nor do I wish to ask for something that is not mine to take. I believe you will find the right queen to sit next to you and care for you, but I do not think it is me. Especially now with these babies in my care. But I will need, how do you say it? A story of how these babies are mine. At least, that is what my ladies suggest. We can somehow answer to why they look like you — perhaps some long-lost cousins you knew nothing about having children before dying, I know not."

"Enough of this! Let's see if we can dig us up a mystery. Oh, Anne, somehow, you bring me such comfort when I am in a foul mood. And certainly, I did not expect to have more children with everything that seems to be against me, especially by God. I would like to see the babies once more after we explore our mystery."

I took Henry to a part of the castle that I rarely frequented. I always found it odd and strange because of how it was kept in such a pristine manner. Books were always aligned in the same place, and nothing was ever out of place. I knew this to be some sort of study room with a library, but it just always made the hairs on my arms stand up. It was a spooky room, but not haunted. I just had no preference for it based on how it made me feel, and I preferred the inner rooms where card games were played, or the gardens.

The whole time I had been there, the sheets still covered the furniture, the books, the desk, and if removed, they would coat the room in a blanket of dust. But I removed one large sheet that covered the chaise lounge and a coffer. Looking at the chaise lounge, I saw that the workmanship was exquisite. I then realized that the Boleyns obviously fancied the French lifestyle. As I studied the lounge, I noticed Henry ran his hand over the softness of the material as if he were reminiscing about something.

"Henry, are you all right? You look lost in thought, or as if you had seen a ghost."

Henry smiled and with a heavy sigh said, "It's just memories that haunt me, nothing more. I loved each of them, but only a few really disappointed me in their duties and affairs. You, Anne, you have always seemed to understand me, though we are from different worlds. But to see this room again.... In fact, when I would pay a visit to Anne Boleyn here, a few times, we would spend our time here with her brother watching. I would come because I would get so mad with her returning my gifts. Then, to see her just sitting there, looking radiant, would remind me I was to marry her. And I did. My sweet Anne gave me Elizabeth, a pride and joy, but not a son. I loved Anne, but then there was treachery by her. I have told no one this, so I must beg you to keep my secrets. After I sentenced her to the tower and to her death, alas, I sent for a French swordsman. The best in the land. I chose a less harsh sentence of death for her, perhaps out of love, perhaps out of pity. Who knew my state back then? It might have been because I loved her. But I grew tired of her, just like I grew tired of young Catherine. I mumble. My apologies, my lady."

I noticed I hadn't moved an inch, listening to Henry, but somehow, he moved to position himself in the lounge. His hands were roaming on the coffer and he flipped the latch, opening it. What we both saw in it shocked us. There were books — many books that looked to be dated, and some actually appeared to be books of heresy. I gasped as Henry reached his hand further into it and pulled out a smaller book, bound by a locket. It appeared to be a journal of some sort. He unfastened the clasp and opened the book. He quickly skimmed the pages and closed the book, handing it to me.

"I can't read this. This is Anne's journal of her secrets and thoughts. I implore you to hold this and give it to my Elizabeth when she is old enough. It should belong to her, as it was her mother's."

I took the book and clasped it in my hands. "It will be my duty to do so, Your Grace."

Henry continued to search the books and pull them out. A lot were books of the Boleyn family and their detailed documents of information. By watching him, I could tell he was very curious about something, but I knew not what caused this. I just simply did as I always had done, listened and showed him he could trust me.

I moved about and pull the sheets off more of the items in the room, and I must have done so quickly because before I knew it, the room looked like one enormous dust cloud. It was so dusty that both Henry and I started coughing. Next thing, we were laughing at my impetuousness in trying to uncover more items in the room.

"Anne! Slow down, woman! If you don't, we are likely to be killed by dust. Evil dust."

I sat down on the floor, laughing so hard. My child-like ways at least could make Henry laugh and ease his moods.

There was one book that was wrapped in a white cloth with a red cross on it, a true marking of the Knights Templar.

Henry's interest was piqued from what I could see. His eyes were enormous as his thick hand reached to pull it out of the coffer. I cleared my throat and it must have distracted Henry, as he looked at me directly.

"The dust, Henry, got caught in my throat. Please tell me what you have there."

Henry's thick fingers unwound the cloth, revealing a book bound by leather, and it looked to be protected from years of dust and damage. Carefully he opened the book and read the words in French, being sure to pause every so often to translate for me. I was so fascinated that I begged him not to stop.

"Anne, this is it. I must read this in its entirety. As this is your home, may I take this book with me?"

"This is one of your castles, though you gifted it to me. It is truly your book. But I ask you to keep me updated on what you read. I am truly in awe with all my learnings since I've come to England. Oh please, Henry, say you'll do that."

Chuckling, he said, "Yes, Anne. It will be our secret, the same with our twins. But as I think about our twins, I make you this promise. They will be yours, but should you or they ever need anything, you only need to ask. I would like to visit from time to time, if you allow."

I nodded and hugged him tightly.

Chapter Fifteen

My Last Battle Days — February 1544
Henry

Though I married Catherine Parr last July in a somewhat quiet, intimate ceremony, this marriage would be my last. I didn't know why, but deep down, I just knew there would be no more queens after her. I spent the time before marrying Catherine in what my beloved sister, Anne, would say as a self-imposed exile. I suppose her words had merit the last time we saw each other in one of my secret visits to her and the children. She cautioned me on my drinking too heavily, for fear that it would upset my poisonous legs or cause me more discomfort. The children were growing in ways so much like me, I secretly gave additional comforts to Anne's household.

I roamed through the halls and as I did so; I heard the court gossiping about what kind of legacy I would be leaving behind considering the young Catherine Howard's infidelities right under my nose. Though Catherine had paid the price for her transgressions, I feared my court was growing weary of me somehow. I sensed betrayal in the air. I would tell my wife of these things, and she would comfort me in her own way and bring me to a sense of calm. Sometimes I would chuckle to her and make a point that of three wives named Catherine, she was so far the most understanding one.

We would talk of many things, but there was one thing I felt I could only trust Anne on. That was to help me with my opinions of politics. So, I sat at my desk and pushed aside all the papers that required my attention and the king's seal, of course. I wrote to Anne instead for her thoughts on something that had been itching at my being.

Dearest Anne,

I write to first inquire about your happiness and that of the young ones. Know that my heartfelt words in this letter should bring you comfort and love. Before I burden you with the main reason for my letter, I hope the young ones that are indeed your true blessing are growing strong and beautiful with each passing day. I think of them often, fondly, as I do you with your sweet lips of wine and that witty way you have with cards. No woman could ever call you a fool for your game of cards!

I need your services, my beloved sister, and after all this time, you are as close to me as Sir Charles. I made an inquiry of Charles V to rekindle our alliance and friendship against France. Pray tell, my sister, that I have your blessing in this, and that I have made a conscious decision that would benefit England and my future heirs, all of them.

I feel I have one last battle in me that would secure my reign in the years to come. If I can, with Charles V, we agreed to keep our alliance so secret that I have not even shared this news with anyone but you and Sir Charles. I can't even trust my Privy Council, but I fear they have spies close to me, so they probably already know. If Charles V and I can take Paris, we will become the greatest of all victors. My sister, I will keep you informed of all matters, but for now, your vow of secrecy is needed. Destroy this letter, but as a reminder of this, accept this gift for you and the young ones. It is a coat of arms that I felt fit your station and beloved nature. Also included are these sweets for the young ones, including Little John.

Your Loving King and Brother,
Henry

I reread the letter to make sure the words rang true, and once satisfied, I called for my personal messenger. He was the only one I would use to send our letters and tokens back and forth. With grave instructions, I handed him the parcels of the gifts I'd collected for Anne and the children, and the letter with my personal seal on it.

"Boy, stay at her side as she reads this, and make sure she understood destroying it afterward. These tokens will provide her the remembrances of my letter. Do as I command, boy."

The boy looked at me and bowed. "Yes, Your Grace. As you command. I will leave straight away."

Returning to my desk, I looked through the papers left to my attention by my council. Some were matters that were alarming—rivalry between neighbors and taxes, among others. Leaving those alone, I opened the trunk I kept locked at all times and took out my secret agreement with Charles V. We sent correspondence back and forth with our personal seals so it would not raise suspicion. We kept our alliance a secret till summer. Come summer, we would plan how we would take Paris and share in the victory. If I went through Picady, and Charles V went through Charlemagne, Francis would have no choice but to give in to a most victorious win. It was pretty ingenious, I would say. A lot of planning was involved.

I laid out the map of France on my desk and made room to study it to offer suggestions to Charles V for his share of the victory. By planning this on my own, I felt young again. Not just that, but I felt vindicated from the prior queen's infidelities. It was as if my spirit lived in that youthful version of myself, just having taken the throne and planning England's future. Through reminiscing, my thoughts moved to the first queen, Katherine of Aragon, and how we envisioned a likeness to "Camelot." But alas, she could not bear me a son that would thrive. Thinking on this drove me to a melancholy moment that I shook off by shifting my focus to France. The lay of the land was staring back at me with no inspiration until it practically jumped off the page at me.

If Charles V would bring his troops from the east, I could meet him in Paris, perhaps from Calais. This was an interesting turning point. But since we had agreed to keep our newly made alliance secret till summer, I had some time to plan a true plan of victory. But for now, this planning of strategy invigorated me. A new lease on life, I'd say!

While lost among the duties of being king, Catherine bade to enter. She was quiet, proper, and beautiful, while knowing when not to anger me. This pleased me immensely.

"Your Majesty and husband, I would like to request to spend some time with the Lady Elizabeth, and have her educated alongside Prince Edward so I can get to know them better while they teach me the ways of the court. May it please you?"

Without looking up, I nodded, but then realized I should probably look in her direction. "Yes, wife. I would be grateful for you to get to know the children and see to their studies. These days, so many things beg for my immediate attention."

Catherine still waited, and since I could feel her presence, I stopped what I was concentrating on and stood up to greet her like a good husband. She placed her right hand on my cheek and stroked my beard. She obviously found a spot that was ticklish on me, and I laughed as I took her hand away and kissed it.

"Tell me, wife, what is on your mind? There must be something else you need to say or ask. So, say it."

Catherine gently placed her hand on mine once more. "Henry, I thought we might talk about the realm and the reformation situation that is happening amongst the people. Surely they know you have their best interests in mind. I just hear some rumors, that is all, and I didn't want the children to learn of them, but Lady Mary is much older. With all the unrest that goes on, it makes me wonder about your succession. We should, rather you should, take steps to ensure your legacy is intact. Pardon my speaking so decisively."

I ushered her to sit. "Dear Catherine, what I tell you now must remain a secret and not be known to anyone else currently. Swear!"

After she nodded her promise, I told her of the new alliance forged with Charles V to take down Francis. France would then be mine, as it should have been. I didn't forget to include that this would cement my legacy in history, but should I die while in battle, she would serve as regent for the realm and for Prince Edward. I then explained to her that only one other person knew of this, and I could trust her implicitly, as should she.

"Catherine, only the Lady Anne of Cleves knows this besides you. After all, she is my Beloved Sister, a title that she earned truly. I hope if I go to this battle, you will serve as regent for Prince Edward. I know you will ensure the realm and his safety above all else. Should you need guidance for the other matters, like with Lady Elizabeth and such, then rely on Lady Anne. I trust you with my boy's life and well-being, should I not return. But if the Lord will be on my side this time, I should ensure the victory of France. Just like I did with Scotland. For I am Henry Tudor, the son of both the White Rose and the Red Rose."

I inhaled as if I just made a proclamation to the entire court instead of just to my wife, but I felt the need for some respect during this time. Too many secrets lay hidden right now that I needed an audience, be it a small one of one person. I kissed Catherine on the cheek and bade her to leave me to finish some ideas I must put together and send word to Charles V. Like a dutiful and proper wife; she returned the affection and told me she would attend to her needlework and other lady amusements.

Pondering once more over the maps and the different

scenarios, I finally found the most competent one to ensure victory. Now to determine how many men might be needed. Part of my plan that would remain unknown to Charles was that I did intend to send many more men than I would tell him. How to pull that off was another question, perhaps for another time, as the puss in my leg leaked through my clothes and I still had matters to consider. This war to invade France was going to be a costly one at that, and I had to increase my treasury for this. I knew I could insist on a benevolence from the people, and there was the gold and silver to be had. Another option was to have several hundred men, at least from the army, raid Scotland—Edinburgh to be exact—but I needed a motivating reason. As I fumbled through some papers on my desk once more, there was a message from one of my spies. God was surely smiling and granting me his favor today. Suspicions from my spy stood out from his letter. Scotland was discussing the possibility of a new alliance with France.

I had no choice but to control the anger that was building inside me, for this was a secret plan of mine. Since the anger matched the level of pain I was feeling in my leg now, I let out a scream and called for the physician.

"Physician, it's the damn leg again. The puss won't stop, and I fear I am going to scream like a woman in childbirth if you don't fix this now!"

The physician rumbled about his things to make a poultice, considering most of the tonics and ointments were in my chambers and we were not. He put together a soothing poultice and placed it carefully on my leg. The stench of the poultice was malignant, but it seemed to do the trick.

My mind was at ease once more, and when he finished, my council appeared before me. The looks on their faces told me they thought me to be dying. Preposterous fools! Only after my land and people, it seemed. Another pain in my heart at the thought that my court wished for my demise and death. I stared right into the eyes of Sir William Petre. I had just appointed him as one of my principal secretaries, but he was the one I trusted the most.

Sir William Petre was a man of average height and build, with dark brown hair and a fashionable build, given his new station probably, and had married Anne Browne just a couple of years ago. Anne served as one of Catherine's ladies-in-waiting. As I watched his body language, Sir William finally gave me the signal I was waiting for. My suspicions were true. Members of this council were not to be trusted. I knew I could trust those brown eyes in my employ. I returned his signal with one of my own, and then he spoke.

"Your Grace, we heard some rather loud noises and came as fast as we could. Is your person all right? Judging by the physician's presence, may we suspect it to be that bothersome leg again and nothing else? For you are in excellent health." He bowed once finished, holding his right arm across the waist. His long black tunic was new, obviously crafted by the lovely hands of his new bride.

"I am fine. It's just this leg again, but as you can all see, I am in excellent health, as Sir William announced. Members of my council, I wish to call a special meeting in four days' time. I will have no need of you till then, so you may go. But Sir William, please stay a moment, as I have some things for you to note. Go now, sirs."

After all others had left, I motioned for Sir William to take a seat while I studied him for a moment. He shifted in his seat, taking every precaution, like in all the other private conversations we'd had. He knew he had earned my full confidence and trust for many years. Having been in my father's service and then in mine, he had earned nothing but my full respect and trust. I shared with him the details about my plan and alliance with Charles V. I then told him I longed to be part of that battle, as it might be my final one to cement my legacy, and that if I went, I wanted him to be part of the group chosen by me to help Catherine be regent. This was a fundamental opportunity for him to stand out among the other members of the council as a trusted man. After all, not only did I knight him, but I made him one of my two private secretaries, and he was the senior of the two.

"Sire, this is truly magnificent. With this approach, you and Charles V will be victorious. But may I suggest something else to add to your legacy? Think about this, if you will, sire. If we could muster up another group of soldiers to follow behind one faction, you might also secure your holding on France should Charles V's army fail or suffer a massive defeat. This group should be behind with enough distance to not be seen as they advance, but be there to show power when the time is right. It may not be needed, but I think this is a sound approach to increase your legacy and power."

I listened as he continued to tell me how the army should take one path over the other and join the first groups when France was under our control. It made sense. The king, with the most soldiers armed and ready to fight, would show the greatest strength to rule overall. It would be a classic, powerful move, and one that I would most definitely enjoy the victory for. I knew I could count on him.

I knew if the time for battle came, he would have to learn the truth about Anne and the children, probably my last two children from any woman, though I dared not admit it to anyone. But now was not the time for secrets to be revealed.

Chapter Sixteen

Beautiful Summer — June 1544
Anne

The growing children always gave me great pleasure whenever I would watch them play in the gardens. Young John Wilhelm and Margaret continued to show their true Tudor colors. As they could now walk and run with a tumble here and there, you could see their heritage, and I recalled being shown pictures of Henry's parents, Henry VII and Elizabeth of York, as well as other members from both houses. There was a resemblance to both houses — the Red and White Rose, you could say, respectively. Remarkably, how much you could see the two houses in these two children. And with my special request to save John Wilhelm, the boy continued to grow strong and healthy, while Margaret continued to show grace and, above all, a strong sense of curiosity to the world around her. Margaret was born with Henry's red hair, but as she grew up, it slowly turned to blonde. Her eyes definitely were heavy lidded, almost resembling those of a dragon. But as she smiled, she had Henry's dimples. When I compared her looks to Henry's mother's line, she definitely resembled the forgotten line of the Yorks. In fact, she was a likeness for Henry's mother, Elizabeth.

The twins were always together, never far apart, and had their own unique twin speak. John Wilhelm would say something, and Margaret would finish. As I watched them play, one of my ladies came running to me.

"Lady Anne, Lady Anne! A letter from the king himself. I came as fast as I could."

Putting down the apple for the twins' snack, I wiped my hands on my skirt. Taking the letter, I noticed the personal seal, not the official one. This was a more personal letter. These were always my personal favorites. I let Lady Jane keep me company, as she had done so many times with these letters. We read the letter together. Taking a deep breath, I told my lady that we must pray for the king's safe return and health. He was going to fight his last battle, a battle that hopefully would give him France to secure his legacy for young Edward. I also noted that he sent his best and loving sentiments to our children, and had kept our secret safe. He did state that if I needed anything and he was in battle, I was to send word to only Sir William Paget, his most trusted and private secretary. He acknowledged he had to share our secret about the young ones to only him to ensure their well-being and mine. I wasn't mad, as I would always be grateful to Henry for his kindness and protection over me, and now with our little ones.

"Lady Anne, do you think the twins can ever be safe

with no one finding out who their father is? I worry about them and you. I feel a sense of protection over you three."

I smiled and hugged my lady. She was always there for me, and I could never forget her kindness as long as I lived. But I did my best to reassure her that the secret would be safe. I continued reading the last part of the letter.

My sweet sister, I say this to you now, in case I shall not return from battle. I am preparing the succession for my throne to be in this order: Edward, Mary, and then Elizabeth. Should anything happen to them, I must ensure my throne's security. With your blessing, I can name John Wilhelm to follow, as he is my true son, or I can look elsewhere for the throne's succession. I know you would not wish to return to court life, so I will leave this decision to you. If you can't send me an answer, send it to Sir William Paget and I will instruct him what to do with it should the answer be yes. You have given me everything I have ever asked of you, and I leave our child's fate in your capable hands. I bear you no ill will, should the answer be no. And you and the children will always be provided and cared for.

A tear trickled down my cheek as I read what I hoped not to be the last letter from Henry. Battles were always tricky and bloody, not to mention there could only be one winner, and the cost was always so high. Men's lives were such a high price to pay to secure land, but it was the way of the world. Upon reading the last paragraph over and over, I glanced at John Wilhelm, and he noticed I was looking at him.

"Mama, mama." He came running over to me and clung to my skirts.

I looked down at him and held his head in both hands.

Then I turned to look at Lady Jane, whispering, "What should this boy's future be? I know the promise I made to spare his life from the curse, but what of the king, his father? He should be honored as well."

"Lady Anne, comfort yourself in his childhood. The king said he would bear no ill will against you. He knows of the promise you made to spare his son. Stay true to your promise, or you will lose this boy for sure!"

"I know. I will write to Henry and his secretary. I will honor my word and promise, but should the land need his last son, it will be the choice of the son when he is of age. I cannot control the son when I am dead, and if he refuses to listen to his mother, but till then, he will know nothing of the succession. But I will make sure he knows his family's history — the history of the Cleves, the Tudors, and the Yorks. For they make this boy and his sister whole. Surely God will accept that and my honor to be a loving servant to him."

John Wilhelm returned to play with his sister, and both children looked happy. Lady Jane eventually gathered them to have their apple and return to the nursery. This allowed me the time to think about their future and what I had hoped for them. Seeing how I asked the curse to spare John Wilhelm and Margaret, as they were twins, I still planned for them to receive the best tutoring and teachings possible, with John Wilhelm focusing on the church, while hoping Margaret would have a happy marriage and one where she could be loved. The challenge would be in them knowing their heritage, but having to keep it secret unless a dire circumstance required they make it known. Hopefully, the latter would never transpire and allow them a life without court. I, for one, had enjoyed being out of the court life.

I took to writing a response to Sir William Paget as Henry requested. I thought long and hard before writing the first word about their future, and how Henry and I wished for the best. And so it began. I politely declined the invitation, if you could call it that, to become part of the line of succession, and wished for a quiet life for them. However, I showed that if the dire need should ever arise, it would be the choice of the son. But till then, I strongly suggested that the son live a life in the service of the Church of England, knowing this was the original path of Henry, and one that he would accept for his son, while Margaret would one day marry a suitable gentleman out of love and not politics. I thanked His Majesty for his kindness to me and the children, and would continue to be his loyal servant. And if anything were to happen to the king, I asked in the letter to be notified. My heart felt full, knowing I could still honor the promise made to the curse.

Even though the twins were only two, it was important to think about their learning path. I asked Sir William Paget if he could suggest possible tutors, that if the truth ever came out about the children once they saw them, the secret could be kept. I would be obliged to cover the costs out of my annual stipend given to me. I just needed proffers to find the right tutor. I also suggested that if it would help the Princess Elizabeth to spend a little while with me with the king's blessing, of course, that I would be honored. A young girl shouldn't worry so when her father was in battle, as boys were much more capable. This might please Henry.

Putting the seal on the letter, I asked Lady Jane to fetch the messenger to deliver this immediately to court. Secretly, I hoped Henry would win over all of France, even be the better over Charles V. I knew this was his calling, his true purpose. There was just something about Henry that made him a strong opponent in any battle.

I checked in on the nursery to see how the little ones were getting by. I'd learned quickly how to be a mother through my ladies and friends that were close to me, and I thought I got the hang of it rather easily. There was something about being a mother that completed my heart. I knew I would not have been this happy if I were to be married. I had everything I could want.

Margaret saw me and came toddling over to me. Her pink dress had a little stain on it from playing in the garden, but I knew she always fussed when having to be changed into new dresses unless it was for bedtime. She hugged me and showed me her doll, a gift from Henry. As I stared into her eyes, she looked back at me with a huge grin on her chubby little face. It was just a baby stage, but as I looked more closely, she definitely reminded me of Henry's beautiful mother. It was also said that his mother looked like her own mother—the two were sometimes mistaken for sisters. She was definitely the white rose, the York.

John Wilhelm tried to run from one end of the nursery to the other, and he had inherited Henry's athleticism at such a young age. These were the closest in resembling the Tudor House. Princess Mary looked like her mother so much, with the dark hair and the Spanish features. Princess Elizabeth also looked like her father. And young Prince Edward, he was a fair skinned boy with so much protection that nothing would happen to him and he could succeed to the throne when the time was right. It was funny to think about it. The children all had their father's features and certain traits, but somehow, they all ended up mirroring their mothers somehow. At least that was my silent observation.

I hugged each child and let Lady Jane know I was going to retire to do some reading. Instead, I wanted some time to reexamine the study that Henry and I explored a couple of years ago to see if I could find any more information about the Tudor history or other distant family members. Not only would this help me to help Henry if needed, but to build understanding for the children. They should know where they come from, even if it must be kept secret.

Entering the room brought back memories of what was, I suppose, the last time Henry really visited and met his children. Taking in a deep breath, I could feel the air rise in and out of my breast. I hadn't really come back into this room since, but at least it had a good airing since then. I left orders to keep this room clean and usable for anyone. Books lined the shelves with care. The globe was positioned by the large window, and even the draperies were drawn open. The sun shone in brightly as ever, and the room was simply magnificent. Scanning the shelves with my eyes, my fingers ran along the edges, hoping a book would jump out at me. Nothing on the first two shelves. Then, as I glanced up, I saw it. I wondered why this book never caught my attention before. There was no writing on it, but a single white rose on the binding. I wondered if this had anything to do with Henry's mother's side of the family.

Immediately I took the book and found a comfortable place to sit, as I knew I would be here awhile. Just think, me, Henry's fourth wife, studying his family legacy. It was just unthinkable, yet here I was with this strange book. My reading of the language had improved, so I should be able to handle this on my own, in secret.

As I opened the book to the first page, I found what I was hoping! For. The first line read, "Because of my mother's agreement with Lady Margaret Beaufort, who liked to be called the King's Mother, I was married to Henry Tudor just last month on 14 January 1486...."

I continued reading.

"The first month married to this Tudor King was both heartache and fascination. I didn't know from one minute if I'd failed him because of who I was, or if I made him somewhat content with my appearance and grace. Though people, including myself, knew I had more right to the crown than he, I sought to find a way for peace and not war. The marriage alliance was to unite the two houses and to stop the years of fighting. If there was any way I could honor my beloved father, Edward IV, then this was it. I was determined to find a way to Henry VII's heart and do my duty. For anyone who shall find this book, this is my personal journey. The journey of a daughter of York, the rightful heir to the throne, though I will support my husband, who won the throne in a decisive battle."

I couldn't believe it. It was here, the queen's diary, I suppose, intact and never having fallen into anyone's hands. I knew there was no way I could get word to Henry about this before him leaving, and that would be an awful distraction for him with what he was planning. I decided I would devote the time he was gone to learning more by reading this book, and sharing it with him when he returned home. It was the least I could do.

Chapter Seventeen

Great Invasion of France — Summer 1544
Henry

I gained a renewed sense of life and strength as we marched steadfast towards France. I had left the French ambassador with the threat of war should Francis not give me the realm I sought. I set about the perilous march as a soldier. A king first, but a soldier with my men with one purpose — to claim France for England. I knew my alliance with Charles V was strong, as we were both united in our goal, but deep down, I wanted France for myself. The air was dry and hot, which was a little unusual for the month, but after the cold winter we had last year, I welcomed the heat because it didn't seem to bother my legs so much. My ambassador had already returned home from Paris, so he was entitled to some time with his wife.

We camped for a couple days' rest, and while the men

were resting, I continued to mull over the battle plans to ensure that things were going smoothly. I felt like I had when I first became king and could do anything. While I savored this thought, without realizing it, my hand clenched and I pounded the table. It caused alarm to my men who were with me, but I recomposed myself, saying, "I haven't felt so alive in years! Men like us should not be cooped up in castles like trapped birds. We need women, action, the feeling of a battle to make us full of life! Hear! Hear!" With that, I raised my cup and honored my comrades. Together we would fight for the glory of England and take France!

We grabbed our goblets and began toasting and drinking, while we laughed and made sure the plans for battle were sound. They had to be. I could not afford a loss as my final battle. I just saw no more battles after this one. I didn't want to think about it, for it would turn my mood melancholy, but it wasn't easy being king. Being a king meant politics and governing, leaving the battles to the army, which a part of me despised because this was where I was my father. Henry Tudor, my father, loved being a soldier more than a king, and that same heart beat in me. Arthur was always the one who was prepared for ruling a kingdom, and how he loved the politics. And to think my own physicians did not want me to partake in such a battle. I had not felt this alive in years with my men. I said, "All right, men, we march along this path, where we should meet Charles V and his men around here. Then, together, we should have about eighty thousand men, a colossal army, to invade Paris—right here." I pointed to the exact spot I planned to take France for myself. I already had extra men waiting in Calais and the surrounding areas. This

time, I had spared no expense for this battle. Secretly, I had
my commanders showing signs to aid Charles V, but not to
use their ammunition and other items. France was going to
be mine. My men lay in wait with about ten thousand men,
just waiting for Charles V to appear, but would then join my
group once we got to Calais. Call it a shadow of force. As
I continued to celebrate with my men, I realized that I had
never felt more alive than I did at that moment.

We continued drinking into the night, and I had to
release all that alcohol that filled my bladder. As much as I
was determined to fit my armor for the march, I was even
more relieved when I had to remove it to release my bladder or
finally go to sleep. I could hear the voice of my one physician,
who was not afraid to voice his opinion while the others kept
silent. "Your Grace, it may not be wise to go to battle with
your men. I fear that should you take part, you may erase
some years you have ahead of you. Your heart and body may
not take the perilous journey. I beg you, for the kingdom's
sake."

I laughed at these thoughts that kept running through
my head. He looked like a canary, but he was a fine physician,
which was why I let him speak freely to me at all times. Being
on the field certainly had its disadvantages with vanity, and
of course, the ladies. Returning to the men, I realized we
needed to pack up camp and get marching. Bellowing orders,
I commanded the men to get a good night's rest and that we
would leave tomorrow. We must get to Paris.

As the men left the tent, I stood outside, surveying the
area. Forty-eight thousand men marched to this plan I had,
and with the carts of weaponry and ammunition we needed,

the horses were aplenty. I listened to the quiet air and realized that we had to make it to the channel in just a short time frame if we were to be victorious. I looked once more at the map before retiring. As I did, I realized it would be easy, like the council said, to take the towns of Boulogne and Montreuil before Somme. I would sleep a few hours before taking one last look, to be sure. I didn't trust my eyes with all the ale I had drunk. But I was relieved I had already sent the Duke of Norfolk, my lieutenant general, ahead with men toward Montreuil. He was to siege the town, allowing my group to focus on Boulogne.

I heard the rumblings of the tents coming down; the men coming to life after our night of drinking, and the horses being fed. I didn't even want to open my eyes until one of my trusted men came to wake me up.

"Sire, the men are eating, but we have been packing up. I looked at the plans once more before coming to wake you. I think we can take the two cities you have marked easily. I am going to send a small group of spies to gather information while we progress. With your approval and command, sire."

I nodded, still drunk, but I knew I had to wake up and lead the men. As I tried to get up, the pain in my leg made itself known. The soldier immediately put together a poultice and applied the pressure without me asking or commanding him to.

"My mother always had to do this for my father, who served in your father's army. I am quite familiar with the remedy. She made sure I would know how in case I should ever have needed it. Allow me, sire. Once I am done here, I will make the spies ready to move out. I swear my allegiance to you to bring you France."

Gritting my teeth together, I could tell this was a different poultice than what I normally had. It didn't smell any better, but somehow, he could make the suffering subside. I told him I could finish while he carried out his plan. I was in full agreement with the approach, and could only hope the men could make it to Paris before Charles V arrived so we could stand against Francis, that perilous idiot of a man.

I had sent Duke Norfolk and Duke Suffolk to begin the sieges at Boulogne and Montreuil. I knew they were capable, and after the council's verdict regarding the plans, I felt they could easily handle both before my men and I arrived there. The towns were going to fall, and once we took control of those towns, we would replenish before moving toward the capital.

As the men and I were ready to set foot on our march, a messenger reached me. The lad looked run down, but I realized he must've ridden the entire way to reach me. Surely, this message must be important.

Taking it from his hand, I found the letter was indeed from the council, affirming that we could easily take Boulogne and Montreuil. They wrote to tell me that the Dauphin regained Montreuil from Norfolk, and that they were on their way already to Boulogne.

Urging the men to march faster, we made our way across the land. Finally, we reached Boulogne, where my men took their rest while I surveyed the fortifications that were in place. I also needed to meet with both Norfolk and Suffolk. I knew this was not the original plan that Charles V and I agreed upon, but I improvised because I listened to instinct that France should only be mine. I had promised forty thousand men, but I secretly had more men at the arm to fight for England. I was angered by Charles's lack of foresight.

"Norfolk, prepare to increase the fortifications. Use what we have and strengthen them. I want Boulogne to crumble and come crawling to me on their knees. They will surrender even if I have to hold them hostage for months. They will fall to the king of England! Considering you failed miserably at Montreuil."

We held the town for two months. God, it was nearly mid-September already. Observing the town, I could see it was certainly taking its toll. We were strong in numbers, and though I had my falling out with Charles V, I cared more for the win. Charles V argued that I did not stick to the original plan, and I argued he did the same. Perhaps this was the line between us I needed to conquer France.

Suddenly, on the thirteenth day in September, Boulogne surrendered, and as I spoke to the town leader, I could feel his homage and his sincerity. I allowed his people to leave Boulogne with their arms and property, seeking refuge elsewhere. After doing so, I claimed Boulogne as my victory and walked into the town. I wanted to see for myself what I had won and what I had lost. The trumpeters lined the walls, sounding their trumpets as I made my way through the town. Looking high and low, I welcomed those that remained as loyal English subjects. A bit of nostalgia hit me that this might be how my father felt as he roamed through England when he took it from Richard III. Breathing in deeply, I carried that same feeling that my father must've had and held my head high. For I was Henry VII, on my way to conquer all.

I reviewed the victory over the French with this last siege, but as my men told me, it cost me greatly. We'd lost half the men we started out with, making it nearly impossible for me to continue to Paris. While we were discussing the cost, a messenger ran in with urgent news. Urgent and disgraceful news. My alliance with Charles V was over now, and he had realigned himself with the Dauphin of France because his siege of Luxemburg took him longer than expected. The news also included that armed with over thirty thousand troops, the Dauphin was preparing to regain control of Boulogne.

I screamed loudly, but not directly at the men. They knew the news was not good. Looking directly at the Duke of Norfolk, I ordered him to hold the city while I returned to England to announce my control over the town. Norfolk looked perplexed and uneasy.

"You have enough men here to hold the city and prepare for Francis to arrive. The fortifications will hold, and the men who are not injured can make any preparations required. I have faith in my men to hold this city for me. Do not disappoint me."

After holding a mass in Boulogne and letting the people get to know me, I prepared for my departure at once. Of course, it was delayed because of my legs, but eventually, a small guard accompanied me back to England and to the queen.

Chapter Eighteen

A Last Christmas — December 1545
Anne

Christmas was always one of my favorite holidays, and with the twins now being three to enjoy celebrations, I had sent an invitation to Henry using our private messenger system, along with Sadie's sweet breads and other delicious delicacies that he so enjoyed from her. I wanted to see him because I had heard through the court gossip that he was not doing so well. The pain in his legs increased more and more, and the whispers were that he had gotten quite larger in the girth since returning from his last battle. The twins were also at an age that they should at least see their father, if just this one more time, based on what I was hearing.

John Wilhelm continued to take in his father's looks, so much that I didn't even recognize the German in him. But that suited me fine, as he was a lovable little boy and his hair was so much like Henry's. Margaret continued to have a gentle nature, yet her hair had turned even more blonde and lost its redness. As I had been studying Henry's family history all this time, I wanted to share what I'd learned with him, and thought this would be the perfect gift to him for all his kindness, and just for being Henry. What I had done was compiled my notes into a diary, if you will, that would make it special for him. I'd kept this secret all this time.

I finished wrapping his gift, hoping he would accept the invitation. I simply waited. The household was busy tending to the decorations and the nights of cards we had with the townspeople. On those nights, we made sure the little ones stayed tucked in their slumber all night. Lady Jane became my closest lady with the twins because they seemed to take to her when I was not around. But I enjoyed being their mother, and all the responsibilities that came with it.

About a week later, one of my ladies came rushing into the nursery where I was playing with the twins, announcing that we had visitors. But no one expected anyone to come, least of all the king. I gently slapped my hands on my skirt and grinned with delight. I urged my lady to make the children ready to greet their father. The boy looked up at me when I mentioned the word "father," and he seemed to realize who was here. He went to hold Margaret's hand and led the way for my lady to change their clothes. He definitely was a miniature version of Henry, wise in his young years.

I promptly made myself presentable and hurried to greet Henry. He smiled when he saw me and insisted that he could not stay long but wanted to ensure that I was happy and content with my life and the children.

"Sit, Henry. Let's at least talk for a bit because I have a surprise for you. If you will permit me extending such a kindness to you."

He laughed heartily and still maintained that jolliness that people loved so much. Henry sat in one chair and politely asked for food and drink, which I requested. I had brought his gift with me as I left my rooms, and held it out for him.

"Henry, I've found some books in the library room that were a find. As I read them, I captured little parts of them to make this journal keepsake for you. It's a story of your Tudor family history, and I've included you and your children. But know that while each queen, including myself, is mentioned, I never disgraced their name or station. I included a few secret pages at the end involving the twins and our relationship, but they are easily removed. I added them to give your life completeness and joy in reading. Please take my special gift."

He reached for the book and opened the wrapping. I had embroidered on the cover the two roses that started his line, but also to show where he came from. With tears, he held it to his heart and said it will always be treasured. He moved to kiss me, and I let him.

"Anne, listen to me. My heart is heavy. We are growing old. I can feel it. Charles died in August, and my heart is making me question everything. Your kindness toward me is immeasurable. The queen and I are happy, but we are not as close as you and I have become, or how I was with the other queens. I leave her to her womanly things, and she leaves me to be king. It is a union required of her king, and I love her, but I am not a young man anymore.

"I have something for the children. They must be so

big now, and are hopefully minding you. Will you let me see them?"

"Of course, Henry! I could never keep them from you. I was so honored to receive your letters and to learn of the victory of your final battle. I knew you could do it." With that, I called on Lady Jane to bring the children to us immediately.

John Wilhelm immediately saw Henry and cocked his head to the right as if he was studying him. It was delightful, but I could sense that John Wilhelm was trying to make sure he knew Henry, and he somehow did. He marched right up to him and gave him a hug. Margaret copied John Wilhelm and also cocked her little head to the right. Henry just started laughing. Secretly, I watched Henry with the children, and it was nice to see, just like it was years ago. He seemed a natural father. But I noticed what the court gossip was all about, and realized it was not gossip. It was true. He was much larger than the last time I'd seen him.

Henry nodded to one man who traveled with him, a man that was ultimately trusted with this, and motioned for him to come forward.

"Anne, please meet Sir William Paget. He is my private secretary, and the man I most trust after Charles, God rest his soul."

I curtsied to him and he told me not to. Instead, he assured me that the secret of the children would be kept, but should I need anything, all I had to do was ask.

I looked back at Henry and gave him a curious look. "Henry, what is wrong? I invited you here to see the children, but I fear there is something you are not telling me. I wanted you to feel loved after the hard year you have had with France and all."

Henry coughed some and then told me he feared he was getting weaker each month. His physicians may have been right about him going into battle in that it may have shortened his life, but he was determined to live whatever time was left with grace and seeing to England's welfare. He shared the line of succession with me, but asked me once more about the children.

Sadly, I shook my head. But I told them both this. "Should England ever need another heir from your bloodline to save her from her enemies, it will be then that the truth be revealed. But John Wilhelm and Margaret will live a life out of court as much as I can allow to save them. I cannot go against the promise I made."

Henry agreed and hoped that day would never come. He knew he would leave England to Edward, and the line of succession would then be to Mary, and finally, Elizabeth, his three remaining heirs to the throne, but not his only children. Looking at the twins, he showered them with presents. He then told me he was preparing to address Parliament this month for his final speech, and shared some things he was going to address with me and Sir William Paget. As I listened, tears started flowing. I noticed that even Sir William Paget had a tear or two. This was going to be a moving and heartfelt speech.

The children were busily looking through their wonderful gifts. Margaret came up to Henry on her own and wanted to sit on his knee. I took her aside and asked her to sit next to Henry, but Henry assured me that his knees were made for sweet little girls. As he looked at her, he was aghast, but not horribly. "She looks so much like my mother. This is incredible."

I told him I'd found a book that had a white rose on it, and it appeared to be a book written in his mother's hand.

He smiled. "I remember that book. She wrote it while I was growing up, and when she gave it to me before dying, she made me swear to keep it safe because it was the York side of me I could not forget. So, after the fall of the Boleyns and I had this castle emptied of their belongings, I placed the book here, knowing it would be safe. And it was. It was safe, waiting for you to find it and remind me of it. So, Anne, I give you her book. I ask that you hold it until Elizabeth is slightly older, and when she may not hate me once she understands the whole truth of what happened to her mother. Will you do that for me?"

I went to clasp his hand and gave him my promise, knowing I also had a secret kept for Elizabeth from her mother. Call me the bearer of Elizabeth's secrets.

Henry again asked Sir William Paget to hand something to me. It was a present for me. It was quite heavy, but as I placed it on my lap, I untied the ribbon that held the cloth. Opening it, I saw an exquisite plaque of some sort. Looking closely, I saw the letters A and C intertwined. Henry had made me a coat of arms! As I looked at Henry, he told me that Sir William Paget saw several were made exactly like this one, and I could place them in my different residences. This was my new official coat of arms from Henry, himself.

"Anne, I also have something to tell you. It won't be in the official will of mine, to honor your request, but Sir William Paget will find you and provide the children and you with what I will leave after my death. I am not dying today, but I wanted to see you, at least this once, to tell you they will always be my children, and their secret will be kept. I do not intend for you to break your promise, knowing what it cost you, but my sweet sister, I accept them as mine. With that, they will have no title to rule, but between us three, they are a lord and lady in their own right. Take this letter that I leave you today and ensure its safety. It will always protect them and have the king's seal on it for worthiness. Speaking from my heart, Anne, I did not love you in the beginning. You know that. But I have grown to love you to this day. Our love, I feel, has grown true since we parted, and I would not change that. Though our lives are separate, we are united by the children we must keep secret and protect. They will live a Tudor legacy freely, and find happiness.

"Maybe I am getting softer in my old age. Who knows? But know that I truly care for you now, and will till my dying breath. I don't know if I will have the strength to visit again, or if we can risk it with all eyes on me because of my health. But you, Anne, have loved me more than any other wife has by being the truest of friends."

With that, he handed me the letter. I dared not open it, trusting Henry at his word, and I knew that meant more to him than anything else. I almost cried at hearing Henry's true soul speak the words. I loved him just the same and told him so. We had survived so much through the years, and no one could question our friendship, for Henry made sure when he titled me the King's Beloved Sister. If anyone ever thought Henry to be a tyrant, then they did not know the real Henry.

I let him continue to spend time with the children alone

as I went to place the letter in my personal treasure box. When Henry was ready to return to court, the children were all smiles, having spent this time with him. It was the moment I didn't think I could ever regret seeing. I remembered something that Charles Brandon once told me when he brought me to England. "To love the king is to know patience. To be in the presence of Henry and really know his true self is to know happiness." And to this day, it had been proven true. I had not once regretted knowing Henry. I also made sure that the twins always remembered from where they came, for they were the Tudor children of the king, but not acknowledged save by just a few. They could live a life free of court, like I was.

THE END

Having been born and raised in Hawaii, I loved telling stories ever since I was a child about vampires, werewolves, angels, demons, and witches. I was a little girl who loved scary stories, much to my mother's dismay. The scarier - the better. Hawaii was a perfect place for stories until I moved to Seattle. I decided to turn a love for the supernatural into writing stories to see if others would love them as much as I do. Currently, I live in Florida but since I'm a Seattle girl at heart, my stories take place in the Northwest. I continue to write supernatural stories of vampires, werewolves, witches, and more while enjoying the beaches and sunshine.

www.ingramcontent.com/pod-product-compliance
Lightning Source LLC
Chambersburg PA
CBHW020128180626
46810CB00004B/1446